PRAISE FOR
A FORGOTTEN HEART

"A touching addition to the Wind River series set in 1890s Calvin, Wyoming, satisfyingly wraps up the McGraw brothers' saga. I loved the heartwarming unfolding love story. I totally enjoyed this story of forgiveness and second chances and highly recommend it."

—CAROLYN, GOODREADS

"I enjoyed this sweet read full of regrets, romance and danger. It's a easy read that had me eagerly turning the pages."

—CATHERINE, GOODREADS

"I enjoyed each story in this series. This one brings an end to the feud with Quade and sees all the brothers happily married. Could easily revisit this series again."

—APRIL, GOODREADS

"Oh my goodness, such a heart capturing story. Pain from past hurts mix with sweet and fun moments that I couldn't put down!"

—RHONDA, GOODREADS

"Such a sweet second-chance romance with a touch of amnesia and a dash of suspense! And I was so happy to be back visiting the McGraw family again! A tender, emotional read with just the right mix of drama and healing."

—RUTH, GOODREADS

A FORGOTTEN *Heart*

WIND RIVER MAIL-ORDER BRIDES

A Forgotten Heart

Lacy Williams
Traci Summeril

Sunrise PUBLISHING

A Forgotten Heart
Wind River Mail-Order Brides, Book 5

Published by Sunrise Media Group LLC
Copyright © 2025 by Sunrise Media Group

Paperback: 978-1-963372-31-1

This book is a work of fiction. Names, characters, places, and incidents are either products of the author's imagination or used fictitiously. Any similarity to actual people, organizations, and/or events is purely coincidental.

All Scripture quotations, unless otherwise indicated, are taken from the King James Version.

For more information about Lacy Williams or Traci Summeril visit their websites at lacywilliams.net and www.tracisummeril.com.

Cover Design: Sunrise Media Group LLC

Wind River Mail-Order Brides

A Convenient Heart

A Steadfast Heart

A Secret Heart

A Dangerous Heart

A Forgotten Heart

Snowbound at Christmas

All to the glory of God.

"I WILL INSTRUCT YOU AND TEACH YOU IN THE WAY YOU SHOULD GO; I WILL COUNSEL YOU WITH MY LOVING EYE ON YOU."

Psalm 32:8 NIV

"GOD HAS GIVEN EACH OF YOU A GIFT FROM HIS GREAT VARIETY OF SPIRITUAL GIFTS. USE THEM WELL TO SERVE ONE ANOTHER."

1 Peter 4:10 NLT

One

"Hey, McGraw!"

Nick McGraw glanced up at the shout as he guided his horse down the muddy, icy track that was Main Street in the tiny town of Calvin, Wyoming. His dog, Patch, circled the horse, careful to stay clear of its hooves.

Nick's old school chum Ames Lancaster was on the boardwalk outside the leather-goods store, bundled in a coat and red scarf, his black wool derby tucked low over his head.

"What're you doing in town? Don't you know there's a storm brewing?" Ames's eyes drifted to the heavy clouds sinking closer to the tops of the buildings.

Not so different from the heaviness weighing on Nick's chest.

"Business." Nick patted his satchel, the strap looped across his chest, with a gloved hand.

An icy gust sliced through Nick's coat, minuscule snow-flakes stinging his cheeks beneath his hat.

Ames scoffed. "It couldn't wait until this storm clears?"

Not when his family depended on him. "It didn't look so bad when I left."

Nick's oldest brother, Drew, had insisted that the sale contract be finalized at the land office as soon as possible. With Christmas only a little more than a couple weeks away, Nick imagined Drew didn't want to worry about anything—or anyone—causing trouble with the simple transaction. Drew was big on legacy, on protecting and expanding the land their pa had left them.

Nick blinked away the snowflakes gathering on his lashes.

Another arctic blast blew over them, making him shiver. He urged Surrey on.

"Don't get caught out in it!" Ames called out after him.

Ames wasn't joking. Dense moisture thickened the air, promising a dump of snow. Nick would need to finish his errands and seek shelter. Soon.

Normally he looked forward to his trips to town. Seeing friends. Catching up on their lives. But today was different.

How long would it be before he saw town again?

After his business at the land office, he'd be stuck in a winter cabin on the side of a mountain for months. Isolated. With only cows for company.

Children's laughter wafted from the schoolhouse as a few stragglers scurried home. Probably released early on account of the coming storm.

He tried not to look. He really did. But when he passed

the white clapboard schoolhouse, his eyes devoured the snug little building.

He hadn't been inside the new schoolhouse, built after the first had been destroyed by fire almost a year ago. That had been just before his cousin Merritt, the longtime schoolmarm, had gotten married and stepped down.

He'd heard the town had hired a new schoolteacher this past September, but he didn't know who or whether they were filling the position well. All he knew was that the new teacher wasn't him.

For so long he'd dreamed of being the one standing at the front of that classroom—

Nick slammed the lid on those pointless thoughts and nudged his horse faster.

Piano music filtered out into the quiet street from the saloon. A familiar horse hitched outside snagged Nick's attention.

He slowed to a stop.

There was no mistaking the blood bay Thoroughbred standing out like a king among its subjects. It belonged to Heath Quade, a neighbor to the McGraws and a constant thorn in their side. The man had poisoned their family's well months ago, and weeks later, had attempted to reroute the river that flowed onto McGraw land, their only source of water.

Why was the man at the saloon instead of at his ranch with his daughter?

Nick's stomach dropped. It didn't bode well.

He nudged his horse forward, but his gaze stayed on the horse as he rode by.

The man had been a menace ever since Nick's pa had refused to sell his homestead to the greedy rancher decades ago. The man was still targeting the McGraw family, like a wolf hunting its prey.

Maybe it was telling that Quade was at the saloon. Two months ago, he'd suffered a hit to his reputation after his foreman and cowhands had been caught working with outlaws.

All of them had been arrested.

All except for Quade.

It unnerved Nick that Quade had kept his nose clean during that debacle—somehow. Still, whispers in town had finally turned against him. Some of the more prominent ranchers in their county had pulled support from Quade in his position as president of the Cattlemen's Association.

Something like that could make a man furious.

If Nick's gut was right, more than one storm lay on the horizon.

Nick puzzled over the rancher's business in town until he reached his cousin Merritt's house. He reined in his horse and dismounted, shaking snow from his shoulders and arms.

Patch faced the snow-splattered street with a whine. Nick reached down and scratched behind Patch's right ear. "It'll be fine, pup. We'll hunker down at the newspaper office with Ed."

With the snow threatening like this, the half-day's ride back home to the ranch would be treacherous. It would be safer for Nick to stay with his brother Ed and Ed's wife,

Rebekah. They were newlyweds, so it would be awkward, but safer than being caught out in the storm.

Merritt swung open the door at Nick's knock. Both eyebrows flicked up, concern etching her forehead. "Nick? I didn't expect to see you. Everything okay?"

She opened the door wide enough for him to slip inside, but Nick hesitated, pinching his lips together.

He saw the quick flash of what he imagined was disappointment before she smiled.

He'd never told her why he'd returned to Calvin before completing his teaching certificate. She'd never asked.

Nick inhaled and removed his hat. He stepped past Merritt into the warmth of her entryway. "I can't stay. I gotta rush over to the land office but wanted to find out . . ."

Merritt tucked her shawl closer around her and tilted her head.

She was going to make him say it.

". . . whether you'd had an answer to one of your letters." Nick's words tapered off as his attention drifted behind Merritt, toward the parlor and the decorations saturating the house.

"Jack decorated," she explained in a murmur. Her husband was new to celebrating Christmas.

Pine garland swagged along the ceiling and over the fireplace mantel. Perfectly tied bows of red velvet accented the boughs. A large fir tree stood in the corner, draped in strings of popcorn with ornaments of dried apples and starched yarn.

All of it screamed of a joyous season. Joy Nick could not share. Not anymore.

Outside, a gust pelted snow against the window. Merritt's expression softened. "I didn't realize you were in such a hurry to find a wife. It's only been a couple of weeks."

Nick rubbed the back of his neck, his face going hot. She was right. It'd only been a couple of weeks since he'd asked her to write some letters on his behalf, hoping that one or two of her long-distance acquaintances might be interested in corresponding with him.

But in those intervening weeks, he'd had plenty of time to observe his oldest brother, Drew, doting on his pregnant wife, Kaitlyn, and his next oldest brother, Isaac, teaching his adopted sons to carve a whistle. His other brother Ed had been holding Rebekah's hand in church last Sunday, their clasped hands almost hidden in the folds of Rebekah's skirts.

Nick had still seen it.

He didn't begrudge his brothers their happiness. Quite the opposite. But he wanted someone to look at him the way Kaitlyn looked at Drew.

After what'd happened five years ago, Nick had given up on the idea of finding himself a perfect match. But watching his brothers find love had reminded him that man wasn't meant to be alone.

He sighed. He'd figured it'd been a long shot. "I'll be wintering up on the mountain with the cattle. After everything that's happened with my brothers and their wives, I'd prefer it if they didn't have a chance to interfere in this."

Her lips twitched. She knew all of it. Kaitlyn's unexpected appearance, answering a letter from Drew that had been addressed to someone else. Ed's failed attempt at securing Isaac a mail-order bride—romancing Rebekah himself. And then David and Jo's misguided attempt at matchmaking that had resulted in a wife for Isaac.

Nick didn't want a surprise bride.

"You want me to hold your letters?" Merritt asked.

"Better you holding on to them than any of my brothers getting hold of one. That is, if there are any."

Merritt stifled a smile. "Of course there will be letters. You're a good catch, Nick McGraw."

He wasn't so sure.

Footsteps sounded on the front porch, followed by someone stomping the snow off their boots.

Nick quirked an eyebrow. "Expecting someone?"

Merritt shook her head. "No. Since I know you need to leave, do you mind seeing who it is outside while I get something from the kitchen for Kaitlyn? It's a new book for Jo that I'd like to send home with you."

She didn't give him a chance to answer as she disappeared into the kitchen.

He reached for the door just as it swung open. Nick stumbled backward to keep it from knocking into him.

"Sorry, Merritt!" But the woman with snow dousing her black coat and blonde hair peeking out from beneath a lopsided hat didn't sound sorry.

She turned away and closed the door before he could get a look at her face. He felt a beat of recognition, even as she said, "Brrr, the temperature is dropping fast."

She patted away the clumps of snow from her coat, the motion somehow familiar, then peeled off her gloves and shoved them into her coat pocket. "I sent the kids home early today with the snow settling in. It's the last day before break anyway. I hope it was early enough for them to get home."

She turned while unbuttoning her coat. "I really need to talk to you."

Her head tilted up and their gazes collided.

Nick's breath seized in his lungs. He couldn't move, his heart frozen mid-beat.

The overdone Christmas decorations faded away as he looked at the only woman who had ever noticed the real Nick McGraw.

Elsie.

Even thinking her name released a rush of memories from the place where he'd barricaded them. They rubbed against something so tender, so raw within him, that all his nerves fired at once.

Her face paled as she gave a heavy blink—as if she, too, wanted to make sure her eyes weren't playing tricks on her.

A drip of melted snow slipped from her hat. Her hand trembled as she brushed away the drop from her cheek.

His hand twitched, as if it remembered the softness of her skin, her hair, and longed for the connection. He clenched his hands until his nails cut into his palms.

Her jaw slackened before she said, "Nick?"

What was she doing here? In Calvin, Wyoming. At Merritt's house.

The door—his means of escaping this torturous moment—was behind her. He couldn't hear Merritt in the kitchen, but she was only steps away. He didn't want to wait for a book or for anything.

He just wanted out of here.

Elsie fiddled with the pleat of her skirt, the same way she always had when nervous. "What are you doing here in Calvin?"

He forced out the words, though they cut his throat like glass. "I live here."

Moments before reaching her friend Merritt's house, Elsie Atchison had leaned into the wind working against her and shoved the letter deeper into her pocket.

I'd hoped to tell you in person, but I can't wait any longer. I love you.

Love her? How could Arnold Nelson love her? He didn't even know her. Not the real her hidden beneath layers of expectations she worked hard to meet.

Snow soaked through her boots, freezing her toes. She forced them faster toward Merritt's.

She'd left the empty schoolroom, but her feet hadn't turned toward the room she rented in the family home of one of her students. The family had left to visit a far-off daughter for Christmas. The house would be entirely too quiet. Elsie needed to talk through this disaster. Needed to find a solution.

Merritt would help. She was her sister Darcy's friend, Elsie's by proxy. She might even be able to tell Elsie how to fix this mess.

The letter crinkled as Elsie hugged her middle.

Love? How had these letters gotten so out of hand? She'd only agreed to the correspondence to avoid disappointing her parents. She'd known Arnold forever but had never felt that way about him.

The thought of marrying Arnold closed in around her as if smothering her. She wanted to teach. Not marry. Her mother couldn't understand how Elsie felt. Pretended she didn't hear when Elsie brought it up.

Arnold was an attractive, polite gentleman that most women would welcome as a suitor. But his charm did nothing to make Elsie's heart beat faster.

Her classroom was a refuge. It was steady. Day in and day out, *she* planned the day for her students. *She* created the rules.

There, she didn't worry about betrayal leaving her raw and vulnerable.

She reached Merritt's house and climbed the porch but stopped in her tracks. Beside the door sat a beautiful dog with shaggy, spotted fur and intelligent blue eyes.

She held out her hand for the dog to sniff. "Well, where did you come from?"

The dog nuzzled into her hand, and she scratched its ears. She hadn't known Merritt liked dogs.

With a final pat, she straightened and stomped the snow off her boots, then after a short hesitation, opened the front door.

When Elsie had first arrived in Calvin, Merritt had taken her under her wing, insisting they were family. And family didn't stand on formalities like knocking on the front door.

A wind gust blew a dusting of snow across Merritt's floor as Elsie practically tumbled in, almost knocking her friend over. "Sorry, Merritt!" With her shoulder, she rammed the door closed behind her. "Brr, the temperature is dropping fast."

She fumbled with the buttons on her coat while she turned around. "I really need to talk to you."

Elsie's hands stalled mid-motion. It wasn't Merritt behind her.

Her breath stuck in the back of her throat. Whether from surprise or dread, she didn't know.

Nick. Nick McGraw.

The very man who'd broken her heart five years ago.

He looked the same except for the stubble darkening his jaw. And the new shadows darkening his eyes.

Never had she thought she would see the greatest regret of her life again.

He stepped back, eyes narrowing as if she had become a threat simply by walking through the door.

At his reaction, an echo of her old anger rose in response.

Five years ago, he'd given her an ultimatum.

That night flooded back. She could almost feel the way the winter air had sliced her cheeks as she'd watched him mount his horse. He hadn't even looked back as he'd ridden away. Hurt and betrayal had vied for the most awful sort of win.

Now the air sizzled with the bite of that familiar betrayal. Something hot.

"Nick?" She whispered his name, barely audible above the wind rattling the windows.

His eyes narrowed.

Idly, she noticed that his hair had grown over his ears. "What are you doing here in Calvin?"

He didn't move, his face a mask. "I live here."

He lived here? She knew his *family* lived here. She'd arrived in town full of nerves, breathless at the thought of seeing him again. But it'd been months, and she'd never seen him. "You're not teaching?" It was a silly question. She was the teacher in the one-room schoolhouse. But if he lived nearby, that meant he wasn't a teacher after all.

A muscle in his jaw twitched. "You sent the children home early? You're the teacher?"

How could the simple words, spat out like that, sound like an insult?

Elsie's stomach churned. She gripped her wet skirt to keep her hands from shaking and raised her chin so he wouldn't see the way her lips threatened to tremble. "I am."

"What happened in Elk Creek?"

Her chin notched higher. "I left." She refused to admit how things had worked out. Not to him. "When Merritt retired, she let me know of the opening. And here I am." She spread her hands out to punctuate her sentence.

He remained closed off, revealing nothing. She'd never experienced Nick like this. He'd always been open to her. Until those very last moments together . . .

No, she couldn't think about that.

So instead, she cleared her throat. "It's been a busy semester. The Christmas pageant went well." Except for when one of the school board members had come in and demanded his daughter be the lead.

Merritt's voice rang out from the kitchen. "I found it! Sorry, Nick—"

His head jerked to the left, his eyes blinking furiously

as if he'd forgotten where he was, what he was doing here. "I have to go."

"Nick, wait—"

For a moment, Elsie thought he would shoulder her out of the way.

"Move."

She stepped aside, shaken. The Nick she'd known before would never have spoken so coldly.

She called after him as he went out into the blowing snow. "I've thought about what I might say if we ever met again—"

"I haven't thought about you at all."

She barely heard his mutter over the wind, but the words struck her like a blow from a ruler across the backs of her knuckles. Sharp, shooting pain.

Tears gathered. Different tears than before.

The door snapped closed behind him, and Elsie's chest heaved beneath the hand splayed across her chest.

Her strength drained away. She leaned against the hallway wall and slid down.

She heard Merritt's swishing dress stop beside her.

Elsie muttered, "You didn't tell me Nick lived at home."

Merritt stood over her with surprise in her wide eyes. Obviously, she'd overheard some of Nick's parting words. "What happened?"

Elsie couldn't speak. She'd come face-to-face with the man who'd been a part of the worst moment of her life— and it was like opening a box of stuffed-away pain. Everything came flooding back.

Elsie shook her head.

Merritt sighed. "I thought you and Nick had been friends."

Friends? Oh, they'd been so much more than that. But back then, Elsie had wanted to keep things about Nick to herself.

"Obviously, there's more to it."

Elsie swallowed. Hard. She'd never told anyone what had transpired that night . . . and at this moment, she couldn't find the courage to tell her dear friend. What would Merritt think of how naive she'd been? Her mistakes?

Merritt eyed her. "Maybe you should go after him. Smooth things over."

"There's nothing left to say."

Merritt bent down, eye level, serious. "Surely nothing happened that would jeopardize your post here in Calvin."

The tone of Merritt's voice made Elsie's mouth go dry. She looked away.

No, nothing indecent had happened, but appearances mattered. Morality clauses in teacher contracts mattered. And she knew how quickly rumors could spread.

"Nick is good friends with Adair Benson," Merritt said. "One of the school board members."

Elsie's stomach lurched.

"They go shooting together sometimes."

No, no, no. If Nick leaked anything about what had happened, her reputation would be in tatters. Her job threatened.

He wouldn't do that, would he?

The old Nick, the one she'd fallen for five years ago,

would never have betrayed her trust. But she didn't know him anymore, did she?

Elsie sucked in a breath. "I think I do need to go smooth things over with Nick."

Smooth things over? Beg for his discretion was more like it.

Concern passed over Merritt's face as she helped Elsie to her feet. "Would you like me to go with you?"

The letter crinkled in Elsie's pocket as she fished for her gloves. Her reason for coming to Merritt had been forgotten in the shock of seeing Nick again.

She'd have to deal with Arnold's declarations later.

With a jerky movement, Elsie yanked the door open. "No reason for you to brave the storm."

Then she charged into the storm, following Nick's disappearing tracks in the snow.

Two

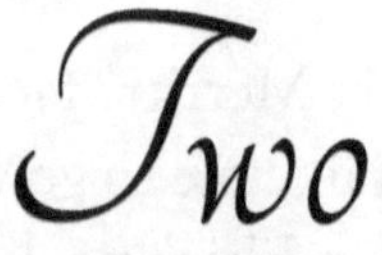

S NOW WAFTED ACROSS THE TOES OF Nick's boots as he stomped down the deserted board-walk, his thumbs hooked around the strap of his satchel, Patch on his heels.

Elsie was a teacher.

Not just a teacher, but *the* teacher in Calvin. Here. The one place he pretended she'd never existed.

It wasn't fair. Nick was the one who'd sat in his small country one-room school building and dreamed of standing at the front of Calvin's classroom. Even in his small school, he'd whispered answers to his seatmate, little Susie Sheridan, and skipped recess to read in one corner of the classroom. He'd tutored the family dog and even the barn cat until the beastly thing had taken a swipe at him.

The gathering drifts along the street insulated him from sound until he heard only his own pulse. And the clamoring of his thoughts.

Nick had been robbed of his dream. Elsie was living it.

He should be happy for her. At one time, she'd shared her own dreams of teaching children to read and learn sums, following in her older sister's footsteps. Back at Kansas Normal School, during her teacher training, Elsie had been so determined. Even . . . desperate to get that teaching certificate.

So why did the discovery hit him in the solar plexus like a brick?

It was seeing her again.

Nick lengthened his stride. At his side, Patch matched his pace, as did the memory of Elsie's doe-like eyes.

They were the first feature Nick had noticed about her five years ago. Back when he'd been delegated as one of the welcome party to greet new students.

The sun had been bright, still hot even though autumn was upon them, and the students at the normal school were milling on the lawn before the start of classes the next day. So many students that he couldn't remember the names of everyone he'd met. Young men and women. He'd felt so mature. Already a year into the two-year program. Halfway to achieving his certificate.

A cool breeze had brushed his face. He'd looked over, and Elsie—he hadn't known her name yet—had appeared on the other side of the lawn, trailing a group of new students. The sun had glinted on her blonde hair, bringing out its red undertones until she almost glowed. She'd looked nervous, fiddling with one of the two textbooks she held against her midsection. She'd been listening to one of the girls speaking in her group, her beautiful eyes taking everything in.

Their gazes locked as the group approached, and the words Nick had said to a hundred other students became sandpaper in his mouth. He hadn't found out until later that he'd somehow recited his welcome speech—she'd discombobulated him that much.

As his partner told the new students about their upcoming schedule, Nick must've been staring, because she ducked her eyes. A simple motion that whisked his breath away.

The group had moved past him, but the rhythm of his heart hadn't returned to normal.

He'd felt an echo of that same breathlessness today before memories of the way things had ended had given him a bitter reminder.

Elsie had never really loved him.

For the first time, the isolation of the winter cabin was appealing. No risk of seeing her in passing there. It wouldn't matter if he missed Christmas. Tillie's birthday. At least he wouldn't be at risk of seeing Elsie.

He didn't stop his march until he reached the land office. A gust pelted snow against his back as he stared at the Closed sign. He was too late. Daniel Freeman, the office commissioner, had already gone. Maybe Nick shouldn't be surprised.

Everyone seemed to have deserted the streets. The saloon was the only store front with any activity, the noisy piano music twanging in the wind. The horses that had been tied to the hitching post out front were gone. Hopefully stabled for the night, somewhere safe. Light spilled from the window. Obviously, there were still patrons inside. Nick was the lone soul braving the storm.

Now what?

Nick glanced at the low clouds. If not for the risk of getting lost in a whiteout, he'd go back to the ranch. Best head to Ed and Rebekah's. He'd promised Drew that he would file the paperwork to complete the land purchase. He couldn't do that until the land office opened back up.

Next to him, Patch stiffened to attention, staring at the saloon across the street.

Nick squinted, trying to see through the snow blowing sideways. The wall of white thickened, shrouding anything past ten feet.

Except for one voice piercing the air. "Nick!"

He'd know that voice anywhere. He tightened his grip on the strap of his satchel as he looked over his shoulder.

Elsie appeared out of the swirling white snow. She staggered but stayed upright. One hand pressed her hat to her head.

The knots in his stomach twisted even tighter.

"Nick, we need to talk."

Talk? She'd ventured into a snowstorm to talk? What a foolish thing to do.

Angry that she'd put herself in danger, he bit off, "There's nothing left to say. Why'd you come out here? You could get lost in the snow."

He saw the tiny flinch she couldn't hide. But her chin came up stubbornly. "I'm not leaving Calvin. I like it here. The children. Being close to Merritt."

So . . . what? As far as he was concerned, the town wasn't big enough for the both of them. Was she going to ask him to leave? That seemed far more gutsy than the Elsie he remembered.

Her shoulders lifted with a sigh he saw but couldn't hear over the howling wind. "I think we should be friends again."

Nick recoiled. He'd never expected to hear those words from her. "Friends? Why?"

"Yes, friends."

The vulnerability in her voice hit him hard, like a punch he wasn't expecting. The pain made him want to lash out at her. "Friends. Like eating meals together and talking about our day?" he asked angrily. "Like sharing secrets and dreams?" Each word he spoke grew harsher. "Or fair-weather friends? 'Cause I've no need for a friend who won't stand by my side when things get hard."

His words weren't fair. He knew it as they left his mouth.

And when she blinked back the tears that pooled in her eyes and averted her face, he felt even worse than before. He should've just walked off.

He started to turn on his heel.

"Don't walk away again." Her voice wobbled, a hint of urgency in her tone.

The reminder of how they'd parted five years ago was another punch. *Choose me. Tell them the truth*. The words he'd spoken so long ago echoed through his mind, heartache chasing them.

"We need to work this out." The plea glittered in her eyes.

There was a time he would've given her everything.

All at once, he was tired. Suffocated by emotions he'd thought he'd gotten over. "Go home, Elsie."

He had to walk past her to get to the newspaper office and Ed. He tried to skirt around her but only took a step before she blocked his path. "Nick, please. If you ever had any real feelings for me at all—"

"If?"

She must've heard the dangerous tone in his voice. He hadn't meant to lean over her, but she'd riled him up until he couldn't think straight. "Elsie, I—"

Patch started to bark.

Elsie jumped. Tears reflected in her haunted eyes, but he still read the fiery determination.

"You couldn't have had real feelings for me," she said. "Not when you were willing to walk away so quickly."

How could she say that? She was the one who'd as much as told him to go.

Patch barked louder.

Nick leveled a gloved finger at Elsie. "You walked away from me first. We can't pretend it never happened."

She gave a long blink, as if she didn't understand him.

It was too difficult to look at her. He couldn't do it without feeling the old tug of attraction, the ghost of what they'd shared between them. And the betrayal that had turned into something bitter on top of all the rest.

"We'll never be friends," he stated. There was no misunderstanding that.

Bang!

Nick startled.

What—

The doorframe two feet behind them splintered, shards of wood flying, as a second bang rent the air.

A bullet.

Elsie's mouth opened in a silent gasp. The moment seemed frozen, jagged, as realization settled.

Someone was shooting at them.

And Nick had only one thought.

Get her to safety.

Another distant crack shattered the stillness. Every cell in Elsie's body jolted. Before she could react, Nick's shoulder rammed into her, knocking her sideways. She lost her footing and stumbled.

Was that—was someone shooting? At them?

She froze, her terrified gaze flitting from building to building, but all she could see was a wall of white snow.

"Elsie, move!" Nick's voice came from close to her ear. With his hand at her waist, he nudged her down the boardwalk.

Go home, Elsie.

Nick's harsh tone from only moments ago echoed in her ears. He had so clearly wanted to be rid of her—but now he was helping her? Pushing her along when she was too frightened to proceed.

Bang!

Beside her, Nick recoiled. For a fractured moment, his hands squeezed her waist.

What was happening? Was he hit? "Nick?"

"Elsie, find cover! Go!"

Hunched over, she tried the closest door, Nick right behind her. Locked. Everything was closed due to the storm.

If she could get to the next street, maybe she could find a place to hide. The step off the boardwalk was right there, so close.

Another bullet splintered the post behind her.

Nick put his right arm around her shoulders and forced her forward, almost knocking her off-balance. "Get down!"

She dropped onto the boardwalk, Nick beside her, his body between her and the shooter.

"Elsie. Go! To the next street!" Gone was the coldness he'd shown earlier, replaced with urgency. Protecting her, even though he didn't have to.

Every muscle trembled, and her hands turned numb. She could barely force herself to crawl forward.

Another shot exploded the snow in front of her. She shrieked.

Almost there, the cross street so close. Elsie could reach out and touch the edge of boardwalk. Nick rose up. As he did, the loudest crack yet split the air from above.

Nick jerked and tumbled backward, collapsing.

Elsie turned in time to flinch at the sickening crunch of his head on the boardwalk's edge as he rolled into the street. "Nick!" No!

She skidded down the step on her belly until she reached Nick. His stillness stole her breath.

We'll never be friends.

She wanted nothing more than for him to open his eyes. To say the cruel, hurtful words all over again.

But he stayed still and so, so pale.

"Help!" she shouted.

Her muscles clenched, waiting to hear another shot—a shot that would pierce her body—but none came.

She scoured the street in both directions. Nothing moved. Everything was a blur of snow, tumbling in all directions, blown by the wind. Where was the man who'd shot at them? Had he gone away?

Did he know that he'd injured Nick? Maybe killed him?

The shooter was still out there. She felt it. Urgency made her next cry louder.

"Help!" But the wind muted her voice.

No one responded. No help was coming.

You walked away from me first.

She was never good at thinking of the right argument in a heated moment—and now it seemed ridiculous that her mind would replay the fight with Nick during this nightmare.

She had walked away from Nick then—but only when he'd asked the impossible of her.

She swallowed against a sob, but it escaped anyway.

Well, she wouldn't leave him now.

Nick's dog hovered nearby, whimpers escaping its throat.

"Go! Go get help!"

The dog yipped twice, then disappeared into the wall of blowing snow.

She had to get Nick out of here. If the gunman came after them, they'd be easy targets. But Nick was six inches taller than her. Solid muscle. She couldn't lift him.

She crawled back up to the boardwalk to a closed storefront and banged her fist against the door.

No answer.

She could barely see Nick's body through the raging blizzard. How long before he froze in addition to his injuries?

She turned toward the next door—the bank. No one would be in there.

Nick needed help. Now.

There was no time to go from door to door hoping someone would answer. The doctor's office was just down the street. If she could get Nick there, he'd be okay. *God, please let him be all right.*

A lump swelled in her throat as she rushed back to Nick, landing on her knees at his side.

We'll never be friends.

Snow dusted his body. She swatted the snow off his coat, then tenderly lifted his satchel off him. She closed the flap that had somehow opened, then hooked the strap over her own shoulder.

He moaned and his eyes fluttered. Was he coming to?

"Nick!"

His eyelids slid closed. She patted his cheek. "Nick, wake up."

He tilted his head away, onto the wound. His eyes flew open as he released a groan through gritted teeth.

He was alive.

But fear choked her. Along with the feeling that whoever had shot at them was still out there.

"Come on, Nick. We aren't too far from the doctor. Get up."

He mumbled something incoherent but still let her help him to his feet. He tipped heavily to one side. Before he fell back into the snow, she wrapped her arm around his waist, steadying him.

He leaned into her. Heavy. "Come on," she whispered. "It isn't far."

He didn't speak. He moaned when she missed a step, and the stumble that barely kept them on their feet jarred him.

Bent low beneath his weight, Elsie trudged through the snow. She prayed the doctor would be in. If he wasn't, she didn't know how Nick would make it any farther. Certainly not back to Merritt's, at the opposite end of town.

Her knees weakened with each step, her boots sliding on the snow and ice. A gust of wind dragged a clump of hair out of her pins and slapped it against her face.

The doctor's office came into view, and she gasped with relief. "Almost there," she panted.

She shifted beneath Nick's weight and stepped up to the boardwalk.

Nick moaned, then crumpled against her. His body weight pinned her to the wall, keeping her upright. Elsie struggled to inhale, the pressure against her chest heavy. They couldn't stop now.

She tapped his back. "Nick."

But he didn't move. Instead, he turned his head, only half conscious, until his breath brushed the hair at the nape of her neck.

"Elsie," he said, his voice low. He mumbled something else she couldn't understand.

Gooseflesh rose on her arms. She clenched her frozen fingers and pounded against the wall.

No answer. She pounded harder, not caring how the impact bruised her frozen hand.

Oh, please be there.

Strength started to fade from her quivering legs as Nick's body became limp.

Slick blood seeped into her coat. How much longer could he continue if she didn't find help?

Their argument didn't matter. He'd flung friendship back in her face, but she didn't care. He needed to survive.

He'd put himself between her and the gun.

Gritting her teeth so tight it hurt, she kicked her heel into the wall. "Hello? Someone help! Please!"

The door flung open. "What on earth—"

Tears blurred Elsie's vision as the doctor lifted Nick's body away from hers. Elsie dragged in a long breath, her weak knees shuddering. "Please. Help him."

"What happened?" The doctor's eyes scanned Nick, already assessing.

Her heart was breaking all over again. "He's been shot."

Three

QUICK. GRAB HIS FEET AND HELP ME carry him inside."

The doctor's voice pierced something inside Elsie and gave her fresh stamina. As she followed instructions, she couldn't stop her gaze from straying to Nick's pale face. There was so much blood pooling beneath him.

Please, God, don't let it be too late.

Together, they carried Nick through the clinic door.

Inside, warmth wrapped around her like an embrace.

The small entryway held two ladder-back chairs. There were two doors, one on each side of the hallway. The walls displayed various certificates and diplomas.

She barely held on to her composure as the doctor led them to an exam room. "You're lucky I heard you. I was just heading out the back to help deliver a baby."

A chill passed down Elsie's spine at how close she'd come to missing the doctor completely.

The rugless room echoed as they hoisted Nick's limp form onto the exam table. She dropped his satchel by the door.

"Put pressure on his shoulder."

She leaned into the rag the doctor had provided to cover the wound and stared at Nick's chest, watching for the rise and fall of his lungs. She found herself breathing with him.

The doctor's mouth pulled tight as he cleaned the wound at Nick's hairline. "How did this happen?"

Elsie swallowed. "He fell from the boardwalk and hit his head on the step."

Something in the doctor's expression kindled dread deep in Elsie's stomach. "He's unconscious because of the blow to his head, not the loss of blood."

But it seemed like so much blood. How bad had the blow been if it was worse?

She drew in a ragged breath. "Will he wake up?"

The doctor didn't answer. Instead, he handed her a pair of scissors. "Here, cut away his shirt. I need to see his shoulder."

As she did, the doctor wrapped Nick's head. The white bandage against his skin gave him a gray pallor.

Grinding her teeth, she refocused on her task, hands shaking. She couldn't injure him further.

The doctor moved to Nick's shoulder, working swiftly.

The vapors from whatever antiseptic the doctor had poured into a rag burned her eyes. She blinked away the blurriness.

The doctor dabbed the wound. "Tell me what happened."

Images of wood splintering just in front of her face, of

the look of shock on Nick's face when he'd been struck, of spilled blood turning the white snow pink—they all replayed in front of her mind, raising her pulse.

The doctor didn't stop working, but he raised an eyebrow, waiting for her explanation.

"We were on the boardwalk, just . . . talking." Arguing. Saying things she'd never say to another living soul. "Then someone shot at us."

The doctor glanced up. "Who?"

Her throat clenched tight. "I don't know. A ghost? I never saw him."

The doctor jerked his head toward a nearby table. "Hand me those forceps." As she did, the doctor's face became thoughtful. "You didn't see anyone?"

"No. It was as if they shot from the sky."

The doctor's mouth tightened. "Or a rooftop." He met her gaze.

A shiver feathered over her skin as the realization hit. It hadn't really sunk in until now.

The streets had been deserted. Someone had to have been aiming for her and Nick.

Elsie gripped the edge of the exam table as her knees went weak.

"You best be speaking with Marshal O'Grady as soon as possible," the doctor mumbled.

Why would anyone want to hurt her? Want to hurt Nick? The violence of it shook her.

Elsie studied Nick's face. Did he have any enemies? It seemed laughable. He'd always gotten along with everyone. Reached out a helping hand.

He'd been a good man.

The doctor probed deeper into his shoulder, but Nick didn't even twitch.

No, she didn't want him to be in pain, but she wanted to see him flinch. Grimace. Anything to prove he was alive. But he lay motionless.

"Got it." The bullet pinged into a metal tray. "After I stitch him up, I've done all I can."

Then what? Just wait for Nick to wake up?

"I have to go deliver that baby."

Elsie's eyes jerked to the doctor. "What?"

The doctor stayed focused on stitching Nick's wound. "I told you I had a baby to deliver. If I don't leave now, I might not make it."

He couldn't leave. Nick was unconscious. What if he didn't wake up?

The doctor snipped away the thread, finished. "The bump on his head is significant. Don't be surprised if he's confused. You'll need to keep him calm. He may wake disoriented."

Shivers nipped at her spine. "But he doesn't even . . ." Like her. Probably outright hated her. "I need to go home."

The doctor pinned her with an intense look. "He has no one but you."

The weight of his words settled.

Nick needed her.

It was so ironic she might've laughed if her insides didn't feel like jelly. "What am I supposed to do?"

The doctor spoke over his shoulder as he bustled out of

the room. "Keep the wound clean. Keep him calm. Don't let him wander into the storm."

The walls echoed with silence.

She hovered at Nick's side. In sleep, with the angry lines around his mouth relaxed, he almost looked like the man she had known five years ago.

Where had the old Nick gone?

With a trembling hand, she lifted a lock of his hair trapped beneath his bandage. "Oh, Nick."

His eyes fluttered open.

With a pinched brow, as if even the dim light hurt, he moved his gaze around the room. Then it landed on her.

She waited for his scowl—the one she'd seen only minutes ago on the boardwalk. But instead, his face softened into a half smile.

Confused, she let her hand drop to her side.

"Elsie. You're here."

Instead of contempt, there was a gruff tenderness that brought back too many painful memories.

She swallowed hard.

He started to sit up but groaned and fell back against the table.

Elsie put her hand on his chest. "You can't get up."

For a second, he looked like he would argue. His eyes closed, then reopened. "I love you."

The words were like a blow to the chest, stealing her breath.

He closed his eyes again, completely out.

He loved her? It wasn't true, she knew it, but that didn't

keep her heart from pounding. She'd believed him once, too long ago.

The doctor bustled into the room and handed her a spare shirt for Nick, which he must've had stashed someplace within the clinic. "Heard voices. Was he awake?"

Her hands trembled as she accepted the shirt. "Just for a minute." She swallowed against the ache in her throat. "He wasn't himself."

The doctor put two fingers at Nick's neck. "What do you mean?"

She couldn't form the words to repeat what Nick had said. "He didn't seem to remember we'd just had a fight. A—a horrible row."

"I've seen tricky head wounds before. Memories can be lost for a period of time. It means there's swelling inside the skull . . ."

The serious look the doctor cast toward her knotted her stomach.

"Will he—will he be all right?"

"It's important he doesn't move around, jar his head again. If he thinks you're on friendly terms, you should be on friendly terms. Keep him still."

She wanted to call after the doctor as he moved toward the door. He made Nick's head wound sound dangerous.

On the threshold, the doctor looked back, black bag in hand and hat pulled low over his eyes. "Whatever you do, don't let him get up and walk around."

And then the door closed behind him.

Elsie wanted to run after him. Instead, she hurried to the

window and scanned the barren street, the spare shirt still clutched in her hands.

The storm had thickened. Of course no one would be out and about. If only someone else could take charge and keep Nick safe. Someone more qualified than her.

But there was no one.

The whitewashed walls shrank in around her, swirling and combining with the white outside.

Friendly terms. She and Nick hadn't been on friendly terms in years.

But they were stranded. Nowhere to go. No help to turn to. Nick's well-being rested solely in her hands.

Oh, what was she going to do?

"Nick. Wake up."

Elsie's dulcet tone reached deep beneath the murky depths of his consciousness and beckoned him toward the surface. But each time he rose closer to where she was, a sharp pain pierced his head, and he relented to the heaviness.

He didn't know the darkness, but he knew Elsie. Sensed she was nearby.

Some time must've passed.

"Nick?"

Nick struggled to emerge from the suffocating darkness. Elsie was calling for him.

But the closer to the surface he came, the greater the pain.

A hand rested on his forearm, warmth against his bare skin. Somehow it soothed the throb in his head.

A faint whiff of lilac met his nose, reminding him of spring and new beginnings.

His lids fluttered open. Even the dim light pierced his temple, and he bit back a groan.

Next to him sat the unfocused image of a woman, dabbing his forehead with a damp cloth. Her lips moved silently. Was she praying? Crying?

Elsie.

His pulse steadied. Her presence flooded a sense of safety over him, and he allowed himself to sink back into oblivion.

Little by little, the pain in his head returned as he awoke again.

Where was Elsie? She was the one thing that had anchored him over the past hours . . . days?

He pried his eyes open, feeling like someone was taking a pickax to the inside of his skull.

The room contained a table next to where he lay, a large cabinet with glass doors adjacent to it. The cabinet contained various surgical instruments and medical beakers. Doctor's office?

Next to him sat a simple wooden chair, but it was empty.

As much as his stiff neck allowed, he scanned the room, but the action triggered his head to spasm.

He cringed. Had he only imagined Elsie earlier?

The low light flickered, making everything blurry.

Then he saw her, standing by the window.

The lantern cast an amber glow over her hair falling in

blond tendrils around her fair face. In the window pane, he saw her reflection looking into the darkness beyond. She nibbled her bottom lip, like she always did when worried.

Something weighed heavily upon her to make her shoulders droop so.

He tried to sift through his recollections, but it was like holding water in his hands. His memories slipped right through.

What was wrong? And why couldn't he remember?

Fatigue pressed down on him, and the ringing in his head lured him to close his eyes again, but he forced them back open.

He shifted, trying to find a more comfortable position, but nothing helped.

Elsie's skirts swished as she turned around. She swiped her hand beneath her eye. Was she crying?

"You're awake."

She didn't seem to look directly at him. Her lips tipped with a ghost of a smile but flattened.

As she lowered into the chair next to him, her hands fisted in her skirts. She appeared tired. Worried.

He tried to reach for her, but a surge of pain locked his arm in place. The movement shifted the blanket around him, and a cool draft swept over his bare chest.

Doctor's office. He must be injured.

Elsie reached over and situated the blanket once more.

"What happened?" he whispered.

Her hands went still, but she didn't look at him. "You don't know?"

Words pressed against his mouth, but pain swelled again in his shoulder, or his head—he didn't know which.

A moan escaped from his scratchy throat.

Her palm covered his forearm. "Shhh. Stay still."

Her presence eased the spasm until he could take in a full breath.

So many questions burned in his gut, but all he could force past his swollen tongue was "Elsie."

He moved his hand to cover hers, but her hand stiffened. With a clearing of her throat, she pulled away to pick up a glass of water on the table next to him.

She held the glass to his bottom lip just before the sweetest water he had ever drunk met his mouth.

"Don't drink too fast," she said. "I don't want you to get waterlogged."

He ignored her and drank like he'd been roaming a scorching desert for far too long.

She pulled the glass away. "I said not too fast."

"So bossy," he mumbled. The corner of his mouth twitched upward, the old tease bringing a moment of lightness.

She pushed a curl of hair behind her ear and lowered herself into the chair again, eyes downcast.

The amber glow of the room embraced her. Candlelight had always enhanced her beauty.

"You are so beautiful."

Red bloomed on her cheeks. He could still make her blush.

But she didn't smile or meet his eyes.

The wind rattled the window, followed by something slamming against the outer wall.

Elsie startled, her attention jumping to the window, hand fluttering to her mouth.

Nick's heartbeat hitched. "What's wrong?"

"Nothing."

She never was a good liar. He probably needed to check it out. He edged up onto his elbows, ignoring the searing heat blazing in his shoulder.

Elsie jumped from her chair, hand on his chest. "Nick, lie down. I'll tell you if you will just be still."

Something had her worked up. She was looking at him at least. Her eyes were shadowed, but he didn't know why. He lowered back down.

"You were shot."

Shot? "By whom?" His head ached as he pressed to remember. Why couldn't he? "Are you all right?" His gaze drifted over her, but he didn't see any injuries.

"I'm fine," she said stiffly.

She wasn't. Something was making her shoulders so tense.

He glanced around the vaguely familiar room. "Where are we?"

"At the doctor's office in Calvin."

"Home for Christmas?"

Her brow creased as if she didn't know how to answer. She rested her hand on the bed next to him, and it was the most natural thing in the world to close his fingers around hers.

But she slipped out of his hold and stood. His thoughts scattered like snowflakes in the wind. "Elsie?"

She blinked hard, then moved back to the window, her arms folded. "Umm, Nick, you hit your head pretty hard. Can you remember anything? Before right now?"

His eyelids drifted closed. His head was pounding, thoughts swirling just out of reach. "I remember how happy we were."

She went still. "Happy?"

He wished he could reach her face and cup her cheek, but his arms weighed a thousand pounds. "Yeah. Do you remember when we were tasked with decorating the commons for Christmas? You were hanging the star on the top of the tree and slipped from the chair, but I caught you. You said, 'I thought you were hanging garland.' And I said . . ."

He waited, wanting the answer from her lips.

Her mouth hardly moved as she said, "'I could never walk away from you.'"

"Or the time we went caroling. I'll never forget it."

Her shoulders hitched and his stomach dropped. What had he said to upset her so? He opened his mouth to ask, but she inserted, "How about anything since school?"

Everything after school stayed behind a thick curtain. Was he even out of school? The harder he tried to think, the more his head pounded.

Maybe that was why he couldn't remember what'd happened this morning. Or yesterday.

At least he remembered the important things.

"Elsie." Nick waited until he captured her gaze with his. "You are the one thing I would never forget."

Her mouth pinched, and she turned away. "Nick, please just rest."

He couldn't understand why she was holding herself distant. The pounding in his head got worse. "My brain may be bruised, but it doesn't change how I love you."

Her gaze flicked to his face, shadows in their depths, but he could no longer keep his eyes open, and he slipped into darkness again.

Four

Y OU ARE THE ONE THING I WOULD *never forget.*

Nick's words rattled inside Elsie's brain long after he'd fallen asleep. His tenderness had taken her off guard, and she was still shaken.

How much longer would this storm last? They'd already been trapped overnight. It was now morning. At least, she thought it was morning. The hours were starting to run together, and the heavy clouds made it difficult to tell.

She sat in her chair and watched him sleep. Gone were the fury and disdain he'd shown yesterday. If she didn't know better, she could almost believe he'd meant those words.

She was going to drive herself crazy.

He didn't love her. He didn't.

The storm beat against the walls. Instead of lifting, it

seemed to have intensified. Low, thick clouds darkened the midday sun.

The walls shrank in around her.

Why had Nick acted so nice when he'd woken up? Like he wanted her there. It muddled her head.

Her heart couldn't handle this. Especially when she knew what was coming. He would wake up, take one look at her, and demand she leave.

She tried to steel herself. Think of something else. Her reputation was on the line. No one but the doctor knew she was stranded with Nick. If the school board found out she'd stayed with an unwed man during the storm overnight, she could lose her position.

The schoolteacher contract she'd signed made it clear that her life must be above reproach. Staying overnight with Nick? It wouldn't matter that he was injured and unconscious. People would talk.

She shivered as cold air seeped in from the corners of the room.

Somehow, she must find someone else to take over as Nick's caregiver.

On the wings of that thought, her stomach released a loud growl. How long had it been since she'd eaten? And what about Nick? He'd been asleep for hours and might wake up hungry. Was there any food to be found?

She got up to look, tiptoeing out of the room. Her footsteps echoed down the empty hall toward the small room in the back of the clinic.

This room had a water pump to the left and a set of cabinets along the far wall. In the corner stood the cast-iron stove. The only stove in the clinic. And rather small for the size of the space.

She hurried to the cupboard and swung open the door. Glass jars containing herbs and tinctures sat inside. She closed it and opened the next. Bandages. Only more of the same. As well as the next and then the next.

Nothing to fill their stomachs.

A chill passed over her. Rubbing her arms, she moved to the tinder box to add a log to the stove. She hesitated. The box was running low as well. It wouldn't be long and they'd need more wood.

No food. No wood. No help.

Her heels clicked on the floorboard as she hurried toward the front window. The drifting snow rippled down the boardwalk in front of the clinic, but a wall of white blocked her view.

If the storm lasted more than another few hours, she and Nick would be in serious trouble.

There was a café across the street, past the town square. It was less than a block away—but it might as well be a mile in a blizzard like this.

What if the owner or a cook had hunkered down at the café? She could find food. And help.

Decision made, she grabbed her scarf and wrapped it around her head and then pushed her arms into her coat sleeves.

She pulled her gloves out of her pocket, now dry but stiff with Nick's blood. She grimaced and glanced over at Nick's coat. Nick's gloves were a much better choice.

She pulled them on but stilled, the felt inner lining familiar against her skin. Not so long ago, she and Nick would take walks together, even in the cold. Once, or twice maybe, she'd forgotten her gloves.

When he'd noticed, he'd taken her hands in his and blown warmth over them before sliding his gloves over her fingers. She could almost feel his hand wrapping around hers. Feel the swoop of her stomach at the warm intensity in his eyes.

She gave a quick shake of her head to rid herself of the memory.

She must hurry. Find help before Nick woke.

Before she could talk herself out of it, she opened the clinic door. A blast of wind caught the door and nearly whipped it out of her hand. She pulled it closed with both hands.

The squall grabbed her skirts and whipped them around like a sail, nearly yanking her off her feet. This was a bad idea. But what choice did she have?

She leaned into the wind and held her scarf with both hands to keep it from blowing away. Trudging toward the end of the boardwalk, she misjudged the end, and her foot sank deep into the fresh powder. It threw off her balance, and she stumbled forward.

The snow whirled around her like a cyclone as she trudged across the street.

She should be nearing the square by now, but all she could see was white.

She looked over her shoulder to judge how far she'd come, but the clinic had disappeared behind a wall of white.

Disoriented, she stilled on the spot, her pulse skittered in her neck. Was she lost?

She searched to the right and to the left. The world had evaporated into a storm so thick she thought it might smother her. Even her footprints had already been covered.

Oh, God. Help.

She moved forward, step by step, until her shins slammed into the boardwalk. She'd made it!

Brown planks of a building materialized out of the white. With one hand on the building, she followed the wall until she came to a door. When it opened, the wind shoved her body through it.

Every muscle fiber shivered as she scanned the shadowed room. Tables and chairs. A serving counter.

The restaurant.

But it only took a moment to register that the building was vacant. Cool air swirled around her feet. It was barely warmer in here than outside.

Some of the tables hadn't been wiped clean, and a few chairs looked as if someone had simply gotten up and walked away. Like they'd been in too big of a hurry to tidy up.

The scent of bread lingered in the air, and her stomach growled.

"Hello?" she called.

No answer.

She wasn't one for fanciful imaginings, but it felt a bit as if she were the only one left in town.

With every limb trembling, she forced her frozen toes

toward the kitchen, her drenched skirts leaving behind her a trail of melting snow.

In the kitchen, she pulled off Nick's gloves and stashed them in her pocket. Her fingers were red and stiff as she gathered flour, eggs, and milk into a sack. At least she could make him some biscuits.

Her hand hovered over a brick of butter, the motion triggering a memory buried in the recesses of her mind. Back when she and Nick had snuck into the kitchen late one night during Christmas break.

Most of the other students had left for the holiday, but she'd lodged at school. It hadn't been until later that she'd learned Nick had postponed his trip home so he could stay with her. No one had ever done something like that for her before.

That night, it'd been his idea to make a meal. She'd chopped vegetables for the stew as he made the biscuits. His calm confidence had entranced her, and she hadn't been able to stop watching his hands as he formed the dough on a pan.

He'd caught her staring, and her cheeks had heated, but instead of embarrassing her, he'd only winked and kept cooking.

After the meal, when they'd been washing dishes together, hands in sudsy water, he'd turned her face to his with a moist knuckle beneath her chin.

And kissed her.

She blinked, the chill of her surroundings whisking her from the memory.

Old grief pressed in around her heart until it broke all over again.

I hope you forget me as quickly as I'm going to forget you.

Nick's furious words from that terrible night echoed in her mind, their sting fresh.

She blinked away the tears and snatched the butter, her movements jerky and a little shaky as she added it to the sack.

The wound on Nick's head would heal. His memories would return, and he'd hate her just as much as before.

She couldn't let herself become confused by his kindness.

Before she left, she found a pencil and paper at the counter and wrote down exactly what items she'd taken along with her name. She would repay the café as soon as the storm broke.

She'd found food, but not the help she sought. What now?

Nick rolled his head from side to side, the words echoing through his dream.

You couldn't have had real feelings for me. Not when you were willing to walk away so quickly.

He'd know Elsie's voice anywhere, but who was she talking to? It couldn't be him, yet the words were familiar.

He would never walk away from her.

Beneath the surface of consciousness, the pain in his shoulder and head throbbed. He didn't want to wake up, but something niggled in the pit of his stomach. Something was wrong.

Words flowed again.

You walked away from me first.

That sounded like his voice, but it couldn't be.

We'll never be friends.

Those words sank in deep and struck a wound he didn't know he had.

He dragged himself into consciousness, forcing his eyes open. Where was Elsie?

"Elsie?" His dry lips cracked as he said her name.

A stab of pain sliced through his head. He raised a hand, and his fingers brushed against a bandage covering his forehead. He allowed his eyes to close. What had happened?

He'd been shot. The knowledge sank in.

He heard Elsie's skirts swish into the room, stop somewhere near.

He gritted his teeth against the pain and peeled open his eyelids. Elsie stood a few feet away, avoiding his eyes, her hands fisted at her sides.

"Are you all right?" she asked stiffly.

He wasn't. The ugly feeling left behind from his dreams swirled in his gut.

"Elsie." He rose up onto the arm that didn't hurt as much. The room started to spin, and he blinked slowly.

Elsie stepped to his side. "Don't get up."

He couldn't if he wanted to, not with being so off-balance.

She pushed gently on his shoulder. "You're going to undo all of the doctor's stitches. Then where will you be? I could hardly watch when he sewed you up the first time."

Sweat beaded on his forehead. "You stayed and watched? You must love me."

She frowned, already moving across the room. "I have some biscuits ready. Stay still." She called the words over her shoulder as she scurried out of the room.

He watched the doorway where she'd disappeared.

Why was she keeping so much distance between them? Acting like she was mad. Or hurt. The angry words swirling through the fog of his brain might be a clue. Had they fought?

Pain pulsed in his shoulder and head as he waited for her to return. He tried to force his brain to make sense of the kaleidoscope of images he'd had since he'd woken at the doc's office the first time.

Why weren't he and Elsie at the family homestead? Where were his brothers?

He could remember a calving season, riding with Ed. Drew scolding him. Isaac playing checkers. Nothing more recent.

She bustled back in carrying a plate with a biscuit. Her eyes focused on the floor. "I'm sorry, but I could only scrounge up ingredients for biscuits. You probably need a stew or soup, but at least you won't starve."

She put the plate in front of where he remained propped on his elbow and retreated a few steps.

He didn't want her to leave.

"How's your family?" he blurted. "I bet Darcy is missing you."

Her jaw stiffened, a sheen glistening in her eyes. Did that mean her parents were once again making demands? "El, they left you over Christmas to go on holiday back east. They shouldn't expect you to be at their beck and call."

Her eyes shot to his. "I'm not at their beck and call. I want to be there for them. Like they were there for me. What's wrong with that?"

He must be a little scrambled in the head. He knew she wanted to please them. Especially her mother. She always said she owed it to them to make them happy, although he never understood why.

Still, he shouldn't have asked a question he knew would be a trigger point. "I'm sorry, El. There is nothing wrong with wanting to be there for your parents. Your kind heart is something I fell in love with."

Her heart-shaped mouth dipped at the corners, a look that always squeezed his chest. But when she bit her lip to keep it from quivering, it about undid him. "Ah, El—"

A giant piece of biscuit was shoved into his mouth. "Why don't you eat and stop talking."

He chewed but didn't take his eyes from her. Even if she did avoid his gaze like she might turn to stone if she met his eyes.

A blast of wind slammed into the window, making it rattle. Elsie whipped her head toward the sound, the plate in her hand trembling.

She set the plate down and moved to the window with arms crossed over her middle, staring outside. Why wouldn't she talk to him? Conversation usually passed so easily between them.

She'd been shy when they first met. He remembered how

he used to do little tricks to get her to talk with him back then.

He tossed his pencil on the floor in front of her as she tried to pass him by in the library. She stopped and stared at it, so he added a ruler on top of it.

Finally, she rolled her eyes and picked up the pencil. She started to hand it back to him, but then she pulled it away and stuck it in her hair, smirking, eyes dancing.

She came to sit with him. Although they talked more than studied.

He didn't have a pencil this time.

He scooted his blanket until it slipped to the floor. She must've noticed, but she remained still.

"I seem to have dropped my blanket."

Her eyes narrowed, and for a moment he thought she would refuse, but she slowly crossed the room. Bent to retrieve the blanket.

Warmth covered him again as she tucked the blanket over him.

He grasped her hand before she could pull away.

She froze, staring at the place where their hands were connected.

She tugged, but he didn't let go.

"Did we have a fight?"

Her exhale shuddered. "You should get your rest."

"El?"

Her fingers trembled as she looked away. "Yes."

No explanation followed.

"Please, El. You're my wife. What can I do to fix this?"

She jerked her hand from his. "Nothing can fix this."

She spun and left the room, leaving him shaken.

He'd pushed too hard.

Whatever had happened must've been big. Elsie was levelheaded and kind. She wouldn't have walls up for no reason.

He didn't know what had passed between them, and trying to push through the blankness to locate the memories only doubled the pain in his head until he had to lie back down.

He didn't know what had happened, but he would do anything to fix his marriage.

Anything.

Because he loved Elsie too much to let her go.

Five

WHATEVER YOU DO, DON'T LET HIM *get up and walk around.* The doctor's warning rang in Elsie's head like an unrelenting school bell. *Keep him peaceful and calm.*

What about Elsie? Keeping Nick calm meant listening to him spout absolute nonsense every time she checked on him throughout the night. Nonsense that was like vinegar on her gaping wounds and broke her heart all over again.

He thought she was his wife? It couldn't be right to let him believe it.

Now this morning, she scrubbed the floor of a second exam room harder, the abrasion of the sponge against the wood matching the rhythm pulsing through her veins.

If he thinks you're on friendly terms, you should be on friendly terms.

Friendly terms were one thing, but this hurt too much.

She must follow the doctor's orders. If something happened to Nick because of shock, it would be her fault.

A sudden realization squeezed her heart, and her scrubbing came to a stop.

Would she have prevented this pain if she'd refused when the doctor demanded she stay?

She touched her pocket, the letter's crinkle a reminder of her parents' expectations. What would happen if she stopped writing to Arnold? Told her parents she only wanted to teach.

Darcy had broken free of Mother and Father's expectations. And Mother hadn't spoken to her for nearly a year. Elsie's stomach pinched. She owed Mother and Father, didn't she?

She shivered. She needed to add another log to the stove. She'd been trying to ration the firewood, but cold was creeping inside.

Wrapping her arms around her torso, she rose to move toward the back room. She stilled when she reached the timber box.

Nearly empty.

"El?" Nick's voice called from the other room.

She added another log to the stove, then slipped into the exam room, bracing herself to see him looking at her tenderly.

Nick was propped on his uninjured arm. "I was about to come find you."

"You'd better not. I can't pick you up if you get dizzy and fall."

He watched her for a long moment—long enough that

she grew uncomfortable and glanced down, only to see goosebumps on the bare skin of his arm.

"I just added another log." But it was chilly in here too. "I'll find more blankets."

She was grateful for the excuse to get out from under his intense gaze, but only found four blankets.

When she returned, Nick was outright shivering. With no wood, he couldn't stay in here. She had to do something.

Before she changed her mind, she rushed to the back room to create a pallet close to the stove, then hurried back to the exam room.

She peeled off Nick's blankets. "We have to move closer to the stove. There isn't much wood left."

Nick propped himself on his elbow. Each muscle quivered as he struggled up.

Her stomach sank. He couldn't move on his own.

She swallowed hard, then slipped her arm around his torso. The feel of him sent a thrill through her muscles.

He teetered slightly as he stood. "I'm a little dizzy." He leaned his muscled side into her and wrapped his arm so that his hand rested on her shoulder.

Strong. Yet tender. The way he'd always been.

She'd not forgotten how it felt to be in his arms. Except, now he was no longer the lean boy on the cusp of manhood. He'd filled out. Grown into his body.

Her heart pounded as they staggered down the hallway. She couldn't reach Nick's pallet quickly enough.

"Tell me about your students this year. Any troublemakers?" he asked, his voice strained.

She needed to say something to take her mind off his

nearness. "I have a girl pulling pranks behind my back. Like sneaking inside during recess and removing the lesson plans from my planner. When I confront her, she acts sugary sweet, saying she would never do such a thing."

"Have you contacted her parents?"

She'd forgotten what it was like to have Nick on her side. The Nick who believed in her when no one else did. "Her father is on the school board, and he told me that picking on the students will not help me retain my position."

Nick tensed. "Why didn't you set him straight?"

"I need this teaching post."

Nick inhaled to speak, so Elsie hurried on before he could. "Then I have another student who isn't grasping geometry. I gave him a triangle equation on his slate and asked him to find x. He actually circled the letter x."

Nick laughed, quickly followed by a grimace. "Don't make me laugh. It hurts."

Elsie smiled. She couldn't help it, even if seeing pieces of the old Nick made her want to cry.

"You're a fantastic teacher, El. He'll get it."

Her ribcage squeezed tight. She'd missed this. Missed him.

They'd reached the pallet she'd made in the back room. She tried to lower him down instead of dropping him like he'd burned her.

The lines around his mouth deepened as he leaned back, his complexion gray.

She started to pull away, but he grappled until he caught her arm. "Stay with me."

An ache swelled deep within her as she pulled away. "I need to get the rest of the blankets."

Once in the exam room, she leaned against the wall, waiting for her breath to stabilize. Only after she could be near him again without falling apart did she return, blankets in hand.

She tried to keep her distance as she spread the blankets over him.

"Thank you," he said. "For taking care of me."

She may be taking care of him, but not with her heart fully intact.

"She is well to look to, thrifty beyond her age. Remember?" His lips tilted in a lopsided smile.

Oh, she knew the reference. Tennyson. But she couldn't let her heart return there. She focused on tucking the corners of the blankets around him. "Not now, Nick."

He shifted restlessly. "What else is there to do?"

Nothing. They were trapped here. But she couldn't play their game, invented when she'd been worried over midterm grades. Couldn't pretend everything between them was good.

"El, you're shivering."

Was she?

He lifted the corner of the blanket, as if he expected her to curl into his warmth. "Come here."

Panic shot through her. "I don't think so."

"Then take one of these blankets. What good is it if you freeze?"

Her breath came in gasps. "I'm not going to take your blankets. You're the injured one."

"Then here." He lifted the corner of the blanket higher.

When she still refused, he said, "If you don't come and lie down next to me or take one of these blankets, I'm going to cast them aside and freeze along with you."

Her eyes widened. He wouldn't do that.

But his raised eyebrows said that maybe he would.

Unsure, she plodded over to his pallet and slowly lay down next to him. He folded the blankets around her, tucking her close to his side. Awareness of his body instantly heated her cheeks. This was so inappropriate. He would be furious with her when his senses returned.

She startled when his arm fell around her shoulders. She should push him away. She should sit up and put as much space between them as possible. But the warmth of his embrace chased away the chill with such force that a tear ran down her cheek.

Outside, sleet pinged against the walls.

"Sweet Lady, never since I first drew breath have I beheld a lily like yourself."

The poem's words wrapped around her chest and squeezed.

"I take your silence as you don't know. I win."

It took a moment for her voice to steady enough to speak. "I don't want to play."

A beat of silence. "Fine. I win."

She could almost believe they sat at their tree, the starry sky stretched over them. "Geraint and Enid. Of course."

"Now your turn."

She heard the smile in his voice.

The past was gone. She could never go back. Except for

maybe just a few minutes to chase away the chill trembling her bones. "*The past will always win. A glory from its being far.*"

"In Memoriam," he whispered. His head tipped so that his bandaged temple rested against the top of her head. "*I love thee, tho' I know thee not. For fair thou art and pure.*"

"Delleus and Ettarae," she returned.

He didn't love her. He didn't. She had to keep telling herself. This wasn't real.

"Your turn," he urged.

Her heart quaked beneath her ribs. "*I am half sick of shadows.*"

There was a beat before he spoke this time. "Are you living in shadows, El?"

Sometimes she felt like a shadow of the woman she wanted to be. The only time she had ever felt free to be herself had been five years ago. When she'd been with Nick.

The months of correspondence with Arnold could never compare.

She was in a no-win situation.

However it ended, this was going to hurt.

Darkness surrounded him from every angle, until it dissolved into snow. Snow so thick he couldn't see, pressing in from all sides.

He started to run, but the storm trapped him with no way to escape.

He spun in a circle, but his surroundings remained veiled within the white curtain.

The hair on his arms stood on end.

Something was wrong. What?

Silence deepened.

Then the crack of a rifle pierced the air.

Nick gasped and woke to a jolt of pain coursing down his shoulder. His head pulsed as he caught his breath.

A log popped, echoing against the metal encasement of the potbelly stove. The bang resembled a distant gunshot, and his heart thumped.

Beside him, the evenness of Elsie's breath calmed the erratic pace of his heart. She was safe, tucked into his side. So why this sense of urgency?

His heart squeezed as he watched her. Gently enough not to wake her, he lifted the fallen tendril across her forehead and smoothed it away. Love overcame him.

Someone had shot at him. If he was in danger, so was Elsie. The realization brushed something ghostlike against his skin.

In his dream, the shooter had remained hidden behind shadows, yet the shooter had been familiar. The feeling that he was missing something important tumbled in his gut.

He tucked his arm close to his body and shoved away the covers tangled around his feet. Once he'd freed them, he sat straight, but his head spun. The drab colors of the room took on hues he hadn't known existed.

Warmth pressed against his back, soothing the erratic rhythm of his heart.

Elsie.

"Nick, what's the matter? Do you need something?" Her voice was soft from sleep.

He forced a smile. "I'm fine. I need to—"

What? Go protect her against an enemy he'd only seen in his dream?

"Do what, Nick? We're in the middle of snowstorm. It's the middle of the night."

He turned to face her. His eyes wandered over her perfectly arched brows, her high cheekbones, her greenish-hazel eyes with flecks of blue around the irises.

He settled back against his pillow. "You're the only woman I ever let boss me around."

There. He only had a view of her cheek and nose, but he saw the soft smile. It faded too quickly, and the tension flared, growing bigger and bigger as the silence lengthened.

He began to whistle. He probably sounded silly and off-key, but the melody of "O Come, All Ye Faithful" rang out.

"My real pa used to sing that." Elsie whispered so quietly he almost didn't hear.

Nick's tune cut short. "What do you mean your 'real pa'?"

She grimaced. "It's late. Let's go back to sleep."

He shifted so he could see her better. "What do you mean your 'real pa'?"

She was silent for so long that he didn't think she was going to answer, but then she said, "I was raised by adoptive parents. I vaguely remember my real pa singing that when we decorated a tree. That's all."

That's all? "What happened?"

Shouldn't he know about this? Maybe it was also something he'd forgotten. If so, what else was missing in the fog of his brain?

She fiddled with the blanket, clearly agitated. "It was so long ago. It doesn't really matter now. I was four when my mom died." Voice so quiet.

His breath caught in his lungs. "Losing a parent matters, El." A fact he understood all too well. How could he have forgotten they shared this commonality?

She stared at the ceiling. "I don't remember her much. More impressions than anything, but I know I loved her very much. And I remember she loved me."

Nick pictured Elsie as a child. All strawberry-blonde curls and dimples. "How could she not?"

"Not everybody likes me."

His head pounded harder. "What do you mean?"

She sighed. "The Westons, my adoptive parents—well, they aren't the first people I stayed with. After my mom died, my dad was more concerned about running his farm than raising a daughter, so he left me with distant cousins. The Granbys. He told me he would come back for me." She gave an unconvincing shrug. "He never did."

The image of Elsie as a child, watching through the window for her father to come, stung Nick's heart.

He closed his hand over hers. This time she didn't pull away.

"What happened?"

She cringed. "Mrs. Granby resented me from the start. I was only another mouth to feed. She never paid attention to me. I even had to comb my own hair."

The muscles in Nick's neck bunched. "A four-year-old combing her own hair?"

"All I wanted was to be noticed. To curl up in her lap as

she sang to me. Or something. Anything. But no matter how much I tried, I never met her approval. Not to mention she allowed her sons to pick on me mercilessly."

"So how did you end up with the Westons?"

She licked her lips. "I was seven. One of the boys said he wanted to play hide-and-seek. I should've known he was up to something, but I was so excited that he wanted to play with me."

He wound his fingers between hers.

"He took me out to a countryside I had never been to, miles from home, and told me to hide and he'd come find me." A tear slipped down her cheek. "He never came looking."

For a heart-wrenching moment, a veil fell, and Nick could see the broken little girl in the woman before him. The little girl who only wanted to be a part of a family. To have a brother who really did want to play with her.

But then her expression went blank.

When she spoke again, her voice was matter-of-fact. "Mr. Weston was the one who found me. I'd been lost for hours. I was hungry and scared. He tried to take me back, but Mrs. Granby said that she'd forgotten all about me." Her sigh shuddered. "She hadn't even noticed I'd been missing."

Nick shoved himself up on his elbow. He didn't care that his shoulder seized in pain. "El, look at me." He waited until she turned her face to him. Her eyes glittered with unshed tears. "You are anything but forgettable. This woman must've been daft, or wallowing in her own misfortune, I don't know. But I do know that you are worth remembering."

Even if he had forgotten this piece of her.

Shame flooded his veins. He would do better.

Something passed behind her eyes before she looked away. "You're only saying that because you have a head injury."

His stomach knotted at the flash of hurt. "Maybe it's my head injury helping me see things clearly."

Her chin quivered, and he felt it like a punch in the gut.

"I'm so sorry. Have you told me this before and I've forgotten?"

She gave a quick shake of her head as if to rid herself of the emotion. "No, Nick. I never did."

"I'm glad you told me now."

She shrugged slightly and turned her shoulder, declaring an end to their conversation.

He stared at her a little longer.

Even with a fuzzy head, he remembered Elsie as always conscientious, quiet, and smiling, not once hinting that something like this was hidden in her background.

He relented to the throbbing in his shoulder and lay back down, staring at the planks in the ceiling.

Had she never felt safe enough to tell him? That thought churned in his gut until he thought he might be sick.

He knew one thing. He wouldn't give up on her like her father had. Somehow, he would fix their marriage. Earn her trust again. Make her smile.

Her breath had evened out, like she was asleep once again. He studied her, examining how her hair fanned around her.

He let his fingers caress the ends, careful not to wake her.

"I will never walk away from you, El. I love you," he whispered.

Six

THE FIRE BURNING IN NICK'S SHOULDER roused him from a restless sleep. He came to wakefulness slowly, head pounding.

He strained his ears before he opened his eyes. Snow lashed the outer wall, the storm still raging. Daylight leaked into the windowless room from the hall door, so it must be morning.

Clenching his jaw against the pain, he stretched his hand across the blankets for Elsie, looking to pull her close again, but the space was empty.

A chill ran through him as he realized she was gone. Where was she?

He pushed himself to a sitting position. Pain a little less, but head still throbbing. What he wouldn't give for one of Ma's medicinal teas.

Relief washed through him when he found Elsie standing at the potbelly stove, her back to him. She must've heard him, because she said, "You shouldn't be up," without looking his way.

Nick wanted to lie back down, but the pain lancing his shoulder kept him rigid for the time being. "I didn't know where you'd gone."

She bustled over and propped his pillow against the wall behind him, still not meeting his eyes. "If you want the coffee I made you, you'd better sit back, or you'll scald yourself."

He watched as she poured his coffee. Calm and quiet as if the middle-of-the-night conversation hadn't happened. Had he dreamed it? No.

He accepted the cup of coffee she held out to him. "How'd you sleep?"

Her hands flitted to a towel hanging on a chair, her gaze averted. "Fine."

Fine. The word sounded crisp on her lips, as if cutting off any other conversation.

The corner of Nick's mouth dipped. After last night, he'd thought for sure the invisible barrier between them had started to crumble. But she acted as if she didn't even remember their conversation.

The coffee turned bitter in his mouth.

"Do you want a biscuit?" Elsie asked from the stove.

He glanced up, but as he did, a leather case leaning against a chair snagged his attention. Several official-looking papers stuck out from the opening.

"Is that mine?" It looked like the satchel he used to carry books when he left for normal school, but it was so worn.

"It is." Before he even had to ask, she brought it to his side.

He scooted himself higher against the pillow, hiding a wince at the fire in his shoulder, and opened the flap.

Inside there were two books. *Around the World in Eighty Days,* his favorite, and *American Cattle: Their History, Breeding, and Management.* An odd choice. One he never would've chosen for himself. The book must be for a student or another family.

He set the books aside and pulled out the papers.

He unfolded them, his eyes scanning the text.

Deed papers?

They hadn't been filed, but it looked like a land purchase. The hairs on the back of his neck prickled as he read the location. If he was right, it was a plot of land adjacent to his family's homestead.

Pain surged into his head, and he closed his eyes.

Why would he be carrying land papers? Was Drew planning to expand the ranch?

Elsie hovered over him. He hadn't even heard her approach. She held out a biscuit, and he took it absently.

He lifted the papers toward Elsie. "El, do you know what this is? Why I've got—"

A loud knock hammered the front door. Elsie jumped.

He watched her eyes dart to the front hall, consider the back door, which was nearer.

"Isn't it still snowing?" Nick demanded quietly. He couldn't forget how jumpy she'd been all day yesterday. Startling at the faintest noise. Someone had shot him. Had they figured out that he'd survived? Come to finish the job?

Elsie stared at the hallway, her cheeks a little pale. "Yes. Still snowing."

Then who was out there? At the door in a whiteout?

Nick wasn't going to let anything happen to Elsie.

He pulled himself to his feet, but dizziness wrapped around him, and he braced one hand against the wall.

Whoever it was banged again.

"Don't answer, El," he whispered. "Maybe they'll think no one is here and go away."

She stood in the middle of the room, indecision written on her expression. "But what if someone needs help?"

Another knock rattled the door against its hinges. "Doctor!" a muffled voice called. "I need a doctor!"

Elsie moved toward the hallway. "We can't ignore someone who needs help." Still, she hesitated.

Nick shoved away from the wall but had to brace his hand again to keep from toppling over. "You aren't going without me."

He trailed her down the hall, ashamed at how weak he was. He was still several steps behind her when she opened the door.

A kid no more than sixteen or seventeen tumbled inside, cradling his right hand wrapped in a rag, eyes wild. "Where's the doctor?"

Elsie stared at the blood staining the kid's towel, brow pinched. "He hasn't returned from delivering a baby."

"I need stitching." The kid looked from Nick to Elsie expectantly. Elsie shook her head, eyes still locked on that bloody bandage.

Nick studied the kid. He didn't look dangerous. "Can't your ma sew you up?"

The boy's eyes roved over the bandage wrapped around Nick's head and down to where Nick's shoulder slumped against the wall. "You don't look so good, mister."

Nick could say the same about the kid. His face was drawn and pale with dark circles under his eyes. Like he'd been up all night. A stab of concern over the kid's situation pricked Nick's stomach.

Elsie must've felt the same. "Come into the exam room."

Inside, Elsie unwrapped the towel from the boy's hand and grimaced, a greenish hue dropping over her features.

Nick shuffled in behind them in time to see the cut was deep. Almost to the bone. The kid really did need stitches.

Elsie covered the wound back up with a fortifying breath. "Take a seat. I'm not a doctor, but I know how to sew."

Of course her compassion would overrule her squeamishness. The kid plopped into a chair as she left the room to gather supplies.

The kid swallowed. "I wouldn't have come 'cept Mr. Quade said I should get stitches."

At Quade's name, a warning shot through Nick's gut. "Quade?"

The kid shrugged. "Sure, he's been there at the saloon since the snow started."

Everything in Nick chilled as if ice traveled through his veins.

An image floated through Nick's mind—an expensive Thoroughbred hitched outside the saloon. Quade's horse. Snow swirling all around.

He tried to focus on the images, but they slipped away, spiraling back into the darkness like a snowflake on the wind.

Was that a true memory? Or his imagination?

"Why were you at the saloon, kid?" Nick asked.

The kid leaned his head back against the chair, as if unaware that his mention of Quade had hit Nick square in the chest. "I work in the kitchen. Mostly washing cups and plates. Mr. Roland let a bunch of cowboys wait out the storm in his place for a price. Mr. Quade was there too. Mr. Roland offered me a week's extra pay if I stayed to keep working. Then a brawl broke out. That's how I sliced my hand."

Nick ground his teeth. So, Quade was waiting out the storm in the saloon with a bunch of drunk cowboys. That couldn't be good.

Elsie hurried back into the room and started to lay the supplies out on the table. She still looked a little green.

She hovered the needle over the kid's hand. Swallowed hard.

Nick leaned away from the wall so he could stand upright. "You can do this, El-Belle."

Something passed over her face. Her gaze darted to his. Nick didn't care that it was the kid needing help who'd prompted her to look at him again. She was finally meeting his eyes, and he tried to use everything inside him to show her the steady belief he had in her. He nodded, and fresh determination settled on her face. As if he'd given her courage.

When she bent over the kid's hand, Nick slumped into a nearby chair where he had a good view of her procedure.

He watched her pinch her lips in determination as she worked, head bowed over the kid's hand. Her fingers were deft and nimble, and she kept stitching with the needle even as the kid whimpered, looking away from where she worked.

As Nick watched her, something niggled in the back of his mind. It wasn't until she snipped the loose thread that he realized her left hand was bare.

His mother's wedding band wasn't on her ring finger. Why wouldn't his wife be wearing his ring?

Nick's head started to throb as Elsie tucked the needle and thread away on the counter across the room. She was saying something to the kid, but her words were muffled as Nick fought off the pain piercing behind his eyes.

He had been up for too long.

There was movement in the room. Elsie bandaging the kid up, maybe? It was all Nick could do to focus on staying upright, one shoulder leaned into the wall.

He did notice when Elsie ushered the kid down the hallway to the front door, using her body to block the view to the back room where they'd slept last night. Why?

Moments passed, maybe longer, before she came back into the room. Her brow creased as she studied him. "Nick? Are you okay?"

He wasn't all right. A wave of fatigue hit, and he let her help him back to his pallet. He slipped off to sleep wondering, where was his mother's ring?

And why couldn't he remember?

The afternoon wore on. No one else sought out the doctor. All Elsie could feel was relief that Nick slept.

You are anything but forgettable.

The words Nick had spoken last night kept haunting her thoughts. Over and over again.

She couldn't keep doing this. Everything inside her wanted to curl into Nick's side. Let his arm come around her shoulders. Press her cheek against his chest. Accept the warmth and comfort he was offering her.

Only, this thing between them wasn't real. His feelings weren't real. And hers were a total mess.

Elsie crossed her arms over her middle, leaned against the doorframe of the exam room, staring out the window.

Still snowing. Snowing hard.

Gusts of wind rattled the window within its pane, and a chill prickled her arms.

That boy from the saloon had made it here. Maybe Elsie could find her way to Merritt's. She tried to map out the streets she'd walk. The blowing snow meant there was virtually no visibility. Could she walk all that way as if blindfolded, playing a game she might with her schoolchildren?

Another night in the clinic wasn't an option. She couldn't repeat the closeness she'd shared with Nick last night.

His affection, feeling his warmth embrace her like a soft blanket she wanted to snuggle into—it'd all stripped her away a piece at a time. Even to the point of whispering things to him she had never shared with another soul.

You are worth remembering.

He'd said the words after she'd told him about her past—something she'd never told anyone else. She rarely unlocked the memories of those days. They were too painful. And Nick's words, spoken with tenderness and compassion, had snuck inside the cracks of her heart.

It hurt so badly. Because it wasn't real. She had to remember this wasn't the real Nick.

The real Nick didn't believe in her. He wouldn't work beside her like a partner. He certainly wouldn't tell her that he loved her.

I will never walk away from you, El. I love you.

Her pulse tripped even thinking about his breath brushing her ear as he'd said those words. He'd thought she was asleep, but she'd been in that nebulous space between wakefulness and drifting off. And then she'd been far too awake to sleep for a very long time.

A shuffling step startled her and tore her from her thoughts just before Nick's hand pressed into her lower back. Her body jolted, and she spun away from him.

She saw a beat of hurt in his eyes as she angled herself away from him. He was standing up. For the second time. He was getting stronger. How much longer before his memory returned?

"I think it's time I go and try to find some help." She spoke over the lump in her throat.

He started to shake his head, but she squeezed past him to the coat rack by the front door. The echo of the words he'd whispered last night was too painful inside her.

"That boy walked three blocks from the saloon. I think I can make it to Merritt's house."

Her limbs trembled so hard it took two tries to shove her arm through the sleeve. But it wasn't from the cold. Nor the idea of being lost in the snow.

It was because Nick was staring at her with such concern.

He tugged the coat, trying to gently take it away from her. "El, it's not safe."

She held fast. She had to do this. "But that boy—"

"Is a kid with no common sense. It'd be easy to get disoriented, lost—you could freeze to death."

She hadn't seen this side of him—fiercely protective—in years. She'd forgotten how it felt to have that care focused on her. Oh, she wanted it.

New tears stung her eyes as he gently pulled her coat back off and hung it on the rack.

"I have to go." She couldn't stay here and wait for him to realize the truth. Her muscles stiff, she turned away and reached for her coat again.

"Fine," he said, a curt tone in his voice. "If you're going, then I am too." He lifted his arm and grabbed his coat, though she saw him wince at the motion.

He couldn't be serious. With his injuries, the storm would suck the life out of him. What if he got dizzy? Fell? She wouldn't be able to carry him back.

"No," she said sharply.

But he ignored her protest. "If you're going, I am too," he repeated.

She knew that stubborn set of his jaw. Knew he wouldn't

back down. She faced off with him anyway. This was his *life* they were arguing over.

"Nick, if you go out there, you could die." The doctor's ominous warning echoed in her mind.

His eyes flashed, dangerous. He edged closer so they were toe to toe. "So could you."

She felt frozen, caught in his gaze. He wasn't going to back down on this. Stubborn man. Her chest locked up tight, the breath trapped there from being so near to him.

His expression shifted, became tender. With the barest of touches, he reached up and brushed a tendril of hair behind her ear, his fingertips caressing her cheek.

"Don't you see, El-Belle? If something happened to you, it would devastate me."

The sincerity in his voice broke through all her walls. Her resolve shattered into a million pieces, and her face crumpled. She couldn't pretend any longer.

Tears trickled down her cheeks.

Nick's hand cupped her face, brushing them away. "Oh, El."

"Stop calling me that." But her words fizzled, mute, pointless. She pressed her face into his hand.

He raised his other hand to cup her jaw. Whispered, "El, please, just let me love you?"

She squeezed her eyes closed, but it didn't stem the flow of tears. Why couldn't she just have this one stolen moment? "You don't love me," she mumbled.

He leaned down, now holding her face between his hands, and kissed one of her tears. "I have always loved you." His lips brushed her other cheekbone. "You're my wife. I would kiss away all of your tears if you would just let me."

He pulled back slightly, and she opened her eyes, looking up into his dear face.

Every memory they'd shared five years ago, every touch, every smile, rushed in all at once, overwhelming her. Before she could stop herself, her hand slid behind his neck, pulling him closer.

He whispered "El" before his lips brushed hers.

She tasted the saltiness of her tears on his lips.

For so long, she'd told herself not to think about him. She'd believed him when he'd said he wouldn't spare her another thought that night he'd ridden away. Maybe he hadn't.

But she couldn't deny that this was the place she always wanted to be. In Nick's arms. His hands closed around her waist, holding her tenderly.

If only she never had to wake up from this dream.

A dream. Not reality.

Her eyes flew open, and she gasped, breaking their kiss. She pushed against Nick's chest, inching away.

What was she doing? Nick would despise her for this when he remembered.

He let her slip away, his face pinched with confusion.

They stood there, facing each other, the sound of their breaths filling the silence.

Her hands came to her cheeks. They flamed hot. How had she let this happen?

"El?"

She couldn't think. She needed distance. Needed her walls back.

With eyes averted, she circled around him to reach her scarf with a trembling hand. "We need firewood. The doctor must have a stock outside somewhere. I just need to uncover it."

Nick didn't say anything, but she was aware of his stare, how close he still stood behind her.

"I'll stay next to the building, in the back alley," she babbled, unnerved. "Surely it has to be close."

They both knew the night would grow too cold to survive if the fire dwindled and died. He stayed where he was as she moved toward the door. Did he feel how much that kiss had unnerved her? Why wasn't he saying anything?

She stopped with one hand on the latch. Couldn't look at him.

He sighed quietly. "If you aren't back in five minutes, I'll come out after you."

She knew he'd keep that promise. She nodded and slipped out into the night.

She hovered for a moment on the stoop, one hand covering her eyes. She'd kissed Nick.

What had she done?

Seven

ELSIE DIDN'T WANT TO OPEN HER EYES. Morning light seeped in from the hallway, but she didn't move. If she was awake, it meant she should separate herself from the steady rise and fall of Nick's chest beside her.

Last night, she'd been completely muddled by Nick's kiss before she'd gone for firewood. She knew she should have pushed him away. Refused the kiss. But there was a part of her that wanted to relive the kiss. Cherish it.

It'd been so much sweeter than what she remembered from their time at normal school. It made her want to laugh and cry all at once.

All too soon, she'd found the firewood stockpiled along the wall at the side of the doctor's office. She didn't have a choice but to go back inside.

Nick stood by the window, coat still on, waiting for her.

It had been a very long time since someone had cared enough to check on her. Wait for her.

He'd offered a boyish smile. "Welcome home."

At his words, something shifted deep inside her.

And she was so tired of resisting.

Next to her, Nick moved, bringing her back to the present. He tugged her closer.

Was this what it would've been like had they never had their fight? This loving, protective Nick, hers forever?

After experiencing what might've been, she didn't know how to put her walls back up.

She opened her eyes. The room seemed brighter. The sun shone in from the front room and carried down the hall to their storeroom.

Outside, a muffled voice called. Someone answered. The sound slithered a cold realization down her back.

The storm was over. The townspeople were out and about.

Feeling suddenly exposed, she forced herself to stand and move down the hall to the exam room, a blanket tightly wrapped around her shoulders.

Out the window, sunlight glistened brightly against the pure white snow. Despite the drifts a couple feet high still blocking most doorways, a smattering of people were out shoveling doorways, sweeping snow into the street.

What if someone needed the doctor and came looking at the clinic? She and Nick would be discovered. Her reputation would be shattered.

She'd known the storm would end, and yet she wasn't ready.

She quickly returned to the back room and bent down next to Nick.

Her hand hovered above his shoulder, ready to wake him, but first she studied his features. This was the Nick she wanted to remember.

It was unfair. *Lord, why have You given me a glimpse of what might have been?*

She swallowed against the lump in her throat and shook his shoulder. "Nick. Wake up. The storm's over."

His eyelids fluttered open, followed by a warm smile. "Morning, beautiful. What time is it?"

She went to the counter and began to quickly clean up the mess she'd made baking biscuits. Her hands shook. "I'm not sure, but people are milling about."

He grunted as he pushed to a sitting position. "We'll need to visit the ranch. My brothers will be looking for me."

She was afraid of that. Nick had three brothers. They would surely be worried about him. Wondering where he'd been. And who he'd been with.

She left the last of the crumbs and grabbed a blanket to fold. "We should pick up. The doctor can't return to this mess." Nor could anyone see their sleeping arrangement. But she didn't voice that.

Nick was slow to stand. "Just give me a moment."

Worried, she set the folded blanket on the floor and went to him.

Careful to not rip open his scabs, she peeled back his bandage. The wound flared red, but no signs of fresh blood. Relief pushed through her.

He was in no condition to ride anywhere. He must've overdone it yesterday. He wasn't going to make it back to the ranch.

He wouldn't thank her to say so.

"There are huge snowdrifts everywhere," she said instead. "You'll want to stay in town a day or two."

He smiled at her with such warmth that her stomach tumbled. "We would sleep a lot more comfortably at the hotel, huh?"

His words hit like a blow, though he didn't realize it. They absolutely couldn't.

Elsie replaced his bandage with shaking hands. "We should go to Merritt and Jack's place."

Merritt would know what to do.

"Merritt and who?"

"Jack. Merritt's husband."

She saw his confusion and consternation in the way his brows drew together. "Merritt isn't married."

"She is married. Since last February." That was why Elsie had come to teach in Calvin—Merritt had given up her post after she'd married.

That knowledge pressed against her chest, but she swallowed the words to tell him. She couldn't admit she was teaching in Calvin without telling him everything.

"We need to go," she reminded him gently. She grabbed his hand and tugged. But he didn't budge.

Instead, he turned her hand over in his and smoothed his thumb over her ring finger. "El, I've wanted to ask, why aren't you wearing my ring?"

He had to have felt her hand tremble, but he didn't let go.

When she couldn't find an answer, he went on. "Drew gave me my mother's ring after she died. I know I gave it to you to wear."

Except they weren't married. And she couldn't bear to lie to him.

She tugged her hand free. "We need to go."

He followed her into the front room, where movement outside the window caught her attention.

She froze.

Outside, a tall man in a cowboy hat crossed the street in their direction. But it was the dog at the man's side that raised her pulse.

Nick's dog.

And they were headed for the doctor's office.

"Nick, someone's coming," Elsie called out.

Nick shuffled into the front room, not sure whether the nauseated feeling churning in his gut was from walking or from the tense tone in her voice.

Maybe he shouldn't have kissed her last night, but she'd responded with such hunger, as if starved for his touch, that he couldn't bring himself to regret it.

And as she'd drifted off to sleep, the way she'd nestled into him had been tinged with desperation.

But this morning, she was acting as nervous as a barn cat brought inside the house.

As he walked into the room, Elsie glanced over her shoulder, her eyes wide when she registered his shirt was still unbuttoned. "Can you button up, please?"

Someone pounded on the door.

Elsie flinched.

He grasped her elbow, not sure yet whether to push her behind him or make a run for it.

The visitor didn't wait for second knock. The door flung open, and a familiar figure stomped in.

"Ed!"

Relief flooded Ed's face as his eyes flicked from Nick to Elsie and back. He took a longer look at Nick, and his expression shifted to concern.

"What happened?" Ed demanded.

Elsie shrank back, but Ed didn't seem to notice as his gaze zeroed in on Nick. He strode forward, flipping the side of Nick's shirt open. "You hurt?"

"Bullet grazed me."

"It more than grazed you," Elsie said quietly.

Ed's attention snapped to her, and his eyes narrowed.

But Nick's focus returned to the door that Ed hadn't closed all the way. The crack in the door widened as a furry snout pushed inside even before the door swung fully open.

A dog with a grayish coat and a spot over one eye trounced to Nick with a whimper, leaving a trail of snow clumps falling from its fur.

Ed leaned in for closer look at the bandage wrapped around Nick's head. "Merritt was worried when you didn't stop by her house to say goodbye. She got Rebekah all riled up. Then, when Patch showed up . . . Who shot at you?"

Ed's rapid-fire questions made Nick's head hurt, and he brushed past his brother to scratch the dog's ears. It nuzzled into Nick's hand, tail swishing.

"Rebecca who?" he asked absently.

Ed seemed frustrated when he turned on his heel toward Elsie. "Who shot at him?"

Nick scrutinized the dog. It seemed so familiar . . . He froze. "Patch. You're Patch." Images of this dog, his dog, flashed across his mind.

Something wiggled loose inside his head, and memories—of teaching Patch to dance on his hind legs, of cuddling the puppy inside his coat on a cold day, of Patch curled on the end of his cot in the bunkhouse—all filtered through Nick's mind.

Followed immediately by a penetrating pain behind his right eye.

He must've gasped, because both Ed and Elsie were right there, each with a hand under his elbow, helping him to stand.

It might've been humorous, the way they stared at each other from either side of him. If his head didn't hurt so much. He pressed one palm into his forehead.

"Start talking." His usually mild-mannered brother must be upset if he was taking that tone. "Who shot at you?"

Nick started to shake his head, then thought better of it. "I don't know. And you were mentioning someone named Rebekah. Rebekah who?"

Ed frowned. "What do you mean 'Rebecca who?' My wife."

Nick's knees weakened, and he slumped against the wall. Wife? His brother was married? "Not Rebecca Edwards. You hate her!"

Ed sent him a slanted look, both angry and worried. "What's wrong with you?"

The memories with Patch still tumbled in his brain, and he couldn't process this new information.

Ed married. To Rebekah Edwards.

Elsie was biting her lip. "You mean the lady who runs the newspaper is your wife?" she asked quietly.

"Yes . . ." Ed drew out, a frown deepening across his features.

Elsie turned her face away. Ed watched her like he was trying to figure out who she was. What was going on?

Nick fumbled for the buttons on his shirt when his fingers wouldn't work right. Ed stood close and buttoned for him. "I knew something was wrong when Patch showed up at the newspaper office."

Elsie was moving around. Picking up again? He couldn't pry his eyes open to see.

"When he was shot, he fell and hit his head." He heard Elsie's voice as if it echoed around an empty chamber. "He's lost some memories."

"Where was he when he was shot?" Ed sounded gruffer than usual.

More rustling from Elsie. "Right when the storm started to pick up, Nick and I were having, well, a discussion on the boardwalk, then someone started shooting at us."

"Who?" Ed barked. He patted Nick's chest when he was finished with the buttons.

"We don't know." Elsie sounded uncertain.

"First, you're missing in a blizzard, then I find out someone was shooting at you." Ed was really riled up.

Nick's eyesight blurred. "Hey, ease up, will ya?"

When he forced his eyes open, Elsie was standing half in

and half out of the doorway to the hall. Nick remembered her urgency last night. She'd wanted to leave to get help. This morning, she'd been ready to leave from the moment he'd woken up. He had a sudden fear that if she left, he would never see her again.

Ed didn't notice. He was staring at the front window. "Quade. It had to be. Him or one of his hired guns."

Nick pushed off the wall, more concerned about Elsie, who'd gone pale at Ed's words. "Quade holed up at the saloon during the storm."

Ed strode to the window and peeked out. "You sure?"

"That's what the kid told us." Hadn't he? Nick's head hurt worse.

Elsie knew. She was watching him. Still poised for flight. "He did."

Ed glanced over his shoulder at her. "What kid? And who are you?"

An expression Nick couldn't identify flitted across Elsie's face. He shuffled toward her, one slow step at a time. "Ed, you know Elsie. My wife."

Ed moved toward Nick, bristling with protectiveness. "Nick, you aren't married."

As if in slow motion, something settled into place in Nick's brain. Elsie was staring back, tears brimming in her eyes.

A muscle ticked in Ed's jaw. "I thought you were the nurse—"

Nick saw Ed's protective, angry words hit as Elsie flinched. He held out one hand to stop his brother. His thoughts whirled, but there was still too much missing.

Ed didn't know Elsie? How could that be?

"The doctor said his memories will likely return. Said to keep him calm so he wouldn't injure himself." The words spilled out of Elsie in a rush.

"So you lied and told him you were married?"

"She didn't," Nick blurted as the realization dawned on him. From the moment he'd come to on that exam table, she'd done her level best to keep him at arm's length. Until that kiss.

Determination rose. Just because they weren't married didn't mean that they didn't love each other. He couldn't have mistaken that. It was there in her touch. In her kiss last night.

He felt it bone deep.

"Leave it," he told Ed.

He still couldn't fathom why Ed didn't know Elsie, but that was a problem for later.

Ed leveled a look on him that said this conversation wasn't over and went back to staring out the window. "I don't like you being so exposed if Quade was the one who shot you. We need to get out of here."

"There are a lot of people out and about. Surely no one would try to attack in broad daylight." But Elsie's argument was more uncertain than anything else.

"You don't know Quade," Ed muttered.

The rancher had been a thorn in their family's side for more than a decade now. Had things gotten so bad he'd taken to outright murder?

Thinking about how close those bullets must have come to Elsie made Nick shiver.

"I can't move fast," he warned his brother. "And we'll be an easy target in a wagon if there's a lot of drifts."

"He can barely walk," Elsie said quietly.

Ed flicked a glance at her and then Nick. "We'll go to the newspaper office for now. We should be safe there until we figure out a way to get to the ranch." He spoke to Elsie as he drew his revolver. "I'll play lookout. Can you help him walk?"

Ed must've somehow known Nick wasn't going anywhere without Elsie. Nick was grateful for that. But Elsie looked like she wanted to protest.

Nick took the last two steps to reach her. "Come with us, El-Belle. You might be a target too. I want to keep you safe."

He saw the flare of her nostrils, the tremble of her lips. This was still the Elsie who'd clung to him last night.

"I'll get your satchel," she murmured, then moved down the hall.

That wasn't an answer. Would she sneak out the back door?

He glanced at Ed, who watched him with a furrowed brow. "What?"

Ed shook his head. "Nothing."

Elsie returned, Nick's satchel looped over her shoulder. Without saying a word, she approached Nick and slid her arm around his torso. She didn't look at him, but that was all right.

They followed Ed out the front door.

This wasn't over. He and Elsie needed to sit down and talk. But first, they needed to get to safety.

Eight

E LSIE HAD ALWAYS FELT A SENSE OF safety when she walked down the street in Calvin. Until today.

She couldn't be sure whether her shivers were from cold or terror as she followed Ed with Nick's arm draped across her shoulders, Patch keeping close behind. Her gaze darted from person to person as townspeople scurried about, digging out from the tall snow drifts.

Who was the shooter? The McGraw men had said it was Quade, but until they knew for sure, it could be anyone.

A reflection glared from across the street. Elsie froze, but it was only a shovel lifted across someone's shoulder.

Bawdy music spilled from the saloon, and she couldn't help scanning the wide second-story balcony. Empty.

Nick's breath had gone shallower. His body was tense, like every step hurt. His face was pale, pain lines bracketing his mouth.

Her legs started to quiver as he leaned more heavily against her.

Glancing back, Ed must've seen them struggling. Without holstering his gun, he dropped back and supported Nick's other side. "We're almost there."

Elsie's muscles appreciated the reprieve even as her gaze clashed with Ed's.

The family resemblance was strong. The same keen gaze. The same cleft in their chin. She could see the fierce protectiveness Ed felt for his brother.

So you lied and told him you were married?

There had been a time when she'd imagined meeting Nick's family. But she never could have imagined the past half hour. Ed's suspicion and fear.

Even now, Ed speared her with narrowed eyes before his attention returned to canvassing the street.

Nick had always said Ed would do anything for family. She saw it in his protectiveness. But he hadn't had any idea who she was.

Nick had made good on his promise. He'd forgotten about her. Never told his family about her.

Her stride faltered, and she stumbled.

Nick tightened his grip around her shoulder. "You okay?"

Elsie regained her balance, but her heart stuttered. "I will be."

Once she was far away from Nick and the McGraw men.

She didn't belong with Nick's family. Didn't belong with Nick.

Their boots hit the boardwalk in front of the newspaper

office, muffled by the thin layer of snow someone had left behind when they'd scooped it.

Ed herded them forward.

Elsie opened her mouth to excuse herself, but when she glanced at Nick, beads of sweat had collected on his now-gray skin.

The short trek had taken a toll. She couldn't leave him. Not yet.

If she saw him settled first, then she'd find a way to go home.

The astringent aroma of ink slammed into her senses as she shuffled sideways through the door. With Nick between them, she and Ed moved behind the front counter and around the large printing press. Stacks of paper and notes were scattered along two nearby desks.

Ed had holstered his gun and now nodded toward the stairs in the back of the room. "We need to get him upstairs." His cheeks had grown pink. From the exertion?

Hurried footsteps sounded on the floor above them. "Ed?"

Elsie recognized the woman who appeared at the top of the stairs. She'd seen Rebekah around town and, as usual, was stunned by the woman's beautiful red hair.

Rebekah's hand came to her chest as she moved toward them. "Oh no. What happened?"

They cleared the top of the stairs, Elsie huffing and ready to collapse.

Ed recounted everything in a dark tone as Rebekah helped them settle Nick on the sofa against the wall. Patch stood nearby, watching with a concerned tilt of his head.

Elsie stepped back as Rebekah pulled a blanket over Nick's shoulders and Ed knelt to pull his boots off.

Rebekah touched Ed's shoulder. "Are you okay?"

An affectionate look crossed his face for a moment. "I'm fine."

That look, the clear love between the two, stirred the what-might-have-beens in Elsie's heart. She wished she could just disappear. Nick was safe now. She should go.

But Nick was staring at her. He shook his head slightly, as if he knew what she was thinking.

Her eyes skittered away and took in the small loft.

Festive decorations brought warmth to the living room. A Christmas tree stood in the corner and poinsettias graced the end table. In the center of the room sat a cast-iron stove radiating a cozy glow, with a small kitchen against the other wall. The scent of cinnamon lingered in the air.

It felt like a home. Not like Elsie's tidy, empty rented room with its lone desk and chair.

"Thank you for helping get Nick here." Rebekah's words jerked Elsie from her thoughts.

Rebekah left the two men at the sofa and moved toward Elsie.

Ed propped a pillow behind Nick's back. "This is Elsie." Was that a hint of annoyance in his voice?

Rebekah's eyebrows rose. "I believe I've seen you around. The new schoolteacher, correct?"

Nick grunted as he twisted his head on the pillow, trying to see past Ed. "The teacher here in Calvin?"

Elsie kept her focus on Rebekah, stomach twisting. "Yes."

Ed cleared his throat. "I think I'll put on some hot water for coffee."

As he passed Rebekah, he stopped for a moment to lean in and whisper something in her ear.

Elsie could only imagine what he might be saying. Then her imagination took flight and provided a vision of her whereabouts splashed on the front page of the paper.

She eyed the stairs. Nick threw off his blanket, earning a harsh protest from his brother.

Nick ignored him. "You're staying put, right?"

Elsie opened her mouth, but nothing came out. How could one look at Nick's earnest, protective expression hurt so much?

"Look at you," Rebekah interrupted. "Skirts soaked to the bone. You must be freezing. Come into the bedroom, and we'll get you warm and dry."

Elsie stiffened. "No, I need to go home."

Nick immediately leaned forward, grunting in pain as he reached for his boot.

"What are you doing?" Ed demanded.

A clank sounded from behind Elsie in the kitchen, but she couldn't look away from Nick, who was clearly trying to tug on his boot.

"I told you I'm going with you." His gaze never left hers.

Rebekah watched everything with narrowed eyes. Everyone in the room knew Nick couldn't make it down the stairs. Elsie knew he was stubborn enough to try, even though he was squinting in pain.

"I don't know why you're teaching in my hometown, and

my head hurts too bad to try and figure it out. But if you leave, I'm going too."

Rebekah looped her arm through Elsie's, breaking the tension in the room. Nick sat back. Elsie had no choice but to give in.

She allowed Rebekah to usher her into a bedroom.

Rebekah bustled to a shelf in one corner of the room. Even with her face averted, Elsie caught her curious expression. "Nick seems very protective of you."

Elsie accepted the towel Rebekah offered her. That hadn't been a question.

She avoided answering by hiding her face in the towel for a long moment. But Rebekah was still there when Elsie lowered the towel, now laying a dress across the neatly made bed.

"Have you known each other long?"

There would be no avoiding this question, not with the pointed look Rebekah aimed at her.

It shouldn't hurt so badly that Nick had never told his family about their whirlwind courtship. She'd kept him a secret too. Even Darcy didn't know the identity of the man who'd broken her heart.

Elsie raised her chin. "We are barely acquaintances."

Not even that. Not anymore.

Rebekah's brows drew together in puzzlement. "But—"

"Thank you for the towel," Elsie said quickly.

Rebekah looked as if she would say something else but then pinched her lips. "Of course."

She left Elsie alone in the tiny upstairs bedroom.

It was only after the door clicked closed that Elsie's face crumpled and she buried her face in the towel.

Everything she'd experienced in the past days poured out in silent tears.

What would Nick tell his family when his memories returned?

Ed and Rebekah were full of questions, and Elsie couldn't give them the answers they wanted. Nor did she want to imagine the anger and disdain on their expressions—an echo of what she'd seen from Nick three days ago.

She needed to leave. But she didn't know how to do that—unless Nick fell asleep. Then she'd excuse herself and go home.

She left Rebekah's dress on the bed and did the best she could to dry her skirts with the towel. She didn't want to go back out there. Face more questions.

But she must.

Nick awakened with a start.

The sunlight streaming through the loft window slanted at a different angle, increasing the throb in his head. Was it late afternoon already?

Where—

It came to him. Ed and . . . Rebekah's? He still couldn't understand how Ed had ended up married to his childhood rival.

He reached down to find Patch curled up on the floor next to him. Where his dog usually lay. How could he remember that but not his brother's wife?

He curled his fingers into Patch's fur, trying to ground his thoughts.

How long had he been sleeping?

Squinting against the light, Nick scanned the room for Elsie. She wouldn't leave, would she?

His eyes landed on her in a nearby chair, asleep with her head tipped to one side.

He released a long sigh and watched her sleeping form.

The sun reflected off her strawberry-blonde hair, strands escaping her braid to frame her face. Her eyelashes fanned across her rosy cheeks, and his heart swelled.

Why hadn't she told him they weren't married? How had she come to teach in Calvin?

Memories teased him from the edge of his mind, as if a nudge would set them all free.

Did he want to know?

A recent memory of Elsie with her face turned away sprang up.

Low voices drew his attention. Ed and Rebekah sat at a tiny kitchen table across the room. He couldn't quite hear what they were saying.

How had Ed and Rebekah gone from sniping at each other during their school days to marriage? And happiness. His head pounded.

Watching the two of them stirred a familiar yearning within him.

Rebekah's gaze snagged on Nick's, and her words drifted away. Ed twisted in his seat.

"Oh, good, you're awake," Ed said as he stood, his chair scraping against the floor. He strode toward Nick.

"Shhh . . ." Nick nodded toward Elsie.

Elsie shifted. Her nose wrinkled, but her breathing remained even. Still asleep.

When Nick tore his eyes away, Ed was standing at his side, watching him intently, brows drawn. Behind him, Rebekah stood from the table and moved to the bedroom.

"You need to be careful," Ed said, voice low. "Not play with this gal's affections. Not if you aren't remembering everything."

This gal? Nick bristled.

But Ed was quiet and serious when he said, "Few weeks ago, you told the family you'd asked Merritt for help making connections with eligible young women."

Ed's words hit and inspired a dissonance like a note being sung wildly off-key.

No. That couldn't be right.

Nick threw off the quilt. Ed must've sensed his agitation, because he put a hand to Nick's shoulder. "Maybe Elsie is one of the women you've been corresponding with."

Nick was already shaking his head. Thought better of it when the throbbing increased. "I've known Elsie since my second year at normal school."

Ed's brows drew together even more. Then his expression smoothed, but his eyes were calculating. "Your second year, huh?"

"What?"

Ed gave a little shake of his head, dismissing the question. "Did you make it to the land office before the storm?"

Nick didn't understand the sudden shift in conversation.

He wasn't finished talking about Elsie. And him seeking a mail-order bride? A sense of wrongness seeped over him.

"I don't remember. I saw the papers in my satchel."

Ed crossed the room to retrieve Nick's satchel from where it'd been left by the stairs.

Nick closed his eyes and rested his forearm over his forehead, putting pressure where it pulsed. A mail-order bride?

He heard Ed rummaging through his satchel, then the sound of papers rustling. It was the change in Elsie's breathing that opened Nick's eyes.

"They haven't been processed," Ed said.

"Why is my name on those papers, anyway? Why not Drew, or you?"

Nick said the words without looking away from Elsie. She rubbed a sleepy hand over her face. Blushed when she realized he was watching.

Mail-order bride? No.

Ed's movements rifling through the satchel became more agitated. "Nick, I can't find the payment."

"What payment?" Nick was distracted from watching Elsie as Ed strode to the table and dumped the contents.

Rebekah bustled out of the bedroom and joined Ed at the table.

"The money, Nick. For the land," Ed said.

He'd had money in the satchel?

Rebekah began sorting through the items next to Ed.

Spots floated in front of Nick's vision as he sat up. "I didn't see any money."

"It has to be here," Rebekah said pragmatically.

Elsie moved to his side as he stood on shaking legs, fighting off the dizziness. Was it his imagination? He sensed she was steadier today.

It was obvious by the tense set of Ed's shoulder they hadn't found it.

Nick's mouth went dry. "How much money?"

Ed shook his head.

Rebekah broke the silence. "Quade was pushing the Spenser family to sell to him. Drew barely convinced them to sell to us."

Quade. Again. The man had tried everything to get his hands on McGraw land.

"If we can't make the purchase, he may swoop in and take it." Rebekah's quiet words were meant for Ed's ears, but Nick heard anyway.

An ugly feeling twisted in his stomach. Somehow, he'd lost that money.

"Could it be at the doctor's office?" Elsie offered quietly.

Her arm curled around his, and he felt a beat of gratefulness for her support.

"Where'd we get that money?" Nick asked. Not a lot of extra cash coming from a working ranch.

"It's part of Kaitlyn's inheritance," Rebekah explained.

Kaitlyn? Who was Kaitlyn?

Something shifted in his mind on another throb of pain.

"Maybe she can make another withdrawal from the bank."

"No one will be able to make it to town from the ranch. Not with the snowdrifts."

"It'll be too late."

Nick watched Ed grow more and more grim as he and Rebekah tried to work through the problem.

"Could it have slipped out of your satchel when you fell?" Elsie offered suddenly.

Dark and hazy memories pressed in. A gunshot. Elsie crying out.

Nick didn't remember falling. Did he?

Rebecca lit up. "If it did, it's buried beneath the snow."

Ed stalked over to the window, his eyes scanning the street below. "Sun will be setting in another half hour. If we go out to find it, we'd better be quick."

"Where were you when Nick fell?" Rebekah asked Elsie.

"In front of the bank."

"The bank."

Nick's and Elsie's words tumbled over each other. Why was she looking at him with that mix of trepidation and hope?

"Did you remember?" she whispered.

"I—don't know."

That particular memory, of stumbling, falling, a flare of pain in his head—seemed clear as day.

"Nick, you've still got a head injury," Elsie said.

"Elsie can show me where," Ed offered.

"No," Nick snapped. Elsie looked shocked by his tone.

"I'll . . . go find your extra pair of gloves." Rebekah disappeared into the bedroom.

"I don't want you going out there," Nick told Elsie, turning so they were facing each other. He clasped her hands in his.

"If it's too dangerous for me, then why are you going?" she countered. "Your head—"

"Is a lot better." It was true. He'd been standing for several minutes without the dizzy spells or nauseated feeling.

"If Quade was holed up in the saloon, he's probably at the bottom of a bottle right now," Ed offered. Nick had almost forgotten he was still standing by the window.

Nick couldn't explain why this was so important, only that it was.

It was his fault that money was missing. He needed to be the one to find it.

And he needed Elsie safe. This business with the mail-order bride, Kaitlyn, the land . . . all of it could wait. And maybe more memories would return.

Elsie was wearing that stubborn set to her mouth—a look that said she wasn't going to back down. He wanted to kiss that look right off her.

Somehow, she read his thoughts. He saw the way her eyes flitted to his lips and then back up. Saw the minute way her lips pressed together. She wanted to kiss him too.

But her gaze cut away as Ed cleared his throat. "We should go."

Nick squeezed her hands to his. "We'll be right back. Wait for me." Then he whistled for Patch to follow him out the door.

Nine

ELSIE WATCHED THE STREET FROM THE second-story loft's window. Rebekah had remained in the bedroom as the men left, and that meant Elsie was left to her own thoughts.

Nick had wanted to kiss her. She was familiar with that intent, fiery look in his eyes. And he'd seen what she'd been too weak to hide—she'd wanted to kiss him too.

Thank goodness his brother had been there. Or maybe that made it more of a disaster.

Nick's memories were trickling back. How much longer before he remembered she meant nothing to him?

Agitation had her turning away from the window.

Rebekah was bustling around in the bedroom. Elsie could see her moving back and forth through the open doorway.

"I'll be just a minute," Rebekah called out.

This was Elsie's moment to make a quiet escape. But her

feet carried her toward the bedroom doorway. What was Rebekah doing?

It hadn't been long since Elsie had been in this room earlier, but now the entire bed seemed to be covered in brown-wrapped packages. Christmas gifts.

A carpet bag sat open on the edge of the bed.

Rebekah was folding up a spare dress. "With everything that's happened, Ed will want to go to the homestead. We'd already planned to be there over Christmas. Now we'll just go earlier than planned."

Rebekah seemed calm, while Elsie was tied up in knots.

Rebekah put the folded dress in the bag. "The McGraws are a close-knit bunch. Nick is especially close with his nieces and nephews. They'll have him singing carols and performing tricks with his dog."

Elsie could easily imagine Nick in the boisterous family gathering Rebekah described. There was a time she'd prayed to be a part of the McGraw family too.

"Will you take the train home for Christmas?" Rebekah looked up from her packing.

"No. Not this year." Elsie's quick answer made Rebekah's brows draw together.

Even before Arnold's letter, Elsie had planned to stay in her rented room after Christmas. Alone.

Back home, the weight of her parents' expectations felt suffocating.

The crinkle of paper in her pocket reminded her of Arnold's expectations too. What was she going to do?

Rebekah moved across the room to a shirt hanging from

a peg, took it down. "You said you and Nick had only just met. I suppose Merritt introduced you."

Rebekah's gently prying words hurt. Elsie had known Merritt for years. They'd met when Elsie was twelve and Darcy had brought Merritt home during a semester break. Merritt and Darcy had inspired Elsie to become a teacher herself.

"No," Elsie said softly.

"No?" Rebekah echoed. "I thought Nick had asked Merritt to help him find a bride—"

She must've seen the words hit. Elsie felt them like a physical blow.

"I'm sorry. I just assumed—"

Elsie whirled, heading straight for the stairs. It was far past time to leave.

"Wait!" Rebekah called out, but Elsie kept on, grabbing her coat from the back of the chair, taking the stairs two at a time.

In all the wild fantasies she'd conjured in the past twenty-four hours—even the most plausible ones where Nick raged at her for letting him get close—she'd never considered he might be courting someone else. Engaged. Smitten.

She burst out onto the boardwalk, the door slamming behind her. She couldn't breathe, not when the cold slammed into her. Not with tears choking her.

She shoved her arms into the sleeves of her coat.

Dusk was falling, only a few stragglers out.

She stepped off the boardwalk and onto one of the shoveled paths tunneling through the drifts toward her rented room, but she slowed to a stop.

She didn't want to be alone in her meager room. She needed to talk to someone.

Wind pelted her in the face, making her teeth chatter.

Merritt. Merritt could help her process the past few days.

She only hesitated a moment on the thought that Merritt was Nick's cousin.

She hurried down the street, conscious of its emptiness. How the snow muffled her footsteps.

She scanned the street as the hair on the back of her neck rose. A gust of wind swirled the snow into a mini cyclone.

Her mind must be playing tricks on her. Replaying the terror she'd lived through. It was not much farther now…

Just before the turn to Merritt's street, she caught sight of two figures. In the distance.

Nick and Ed. They bent over the snow in front of the land office. Patch wandered, sniffing around the snow.

Her heart pinched. This might be the last time she saw Nick.

Patch barked and started to dig at a spot in the snow. Ed said something to Nick, then joined the dog and scooped away snow from the spot.

She licked her wind-chapped lips. "Goodbye, Nick."

She couldn't shake that awful feeling of impending doom. She knew it wasn't real, but she couldn't bear it. She must go.

Just then, Patch began an incessant bark that grabbed her attention.

She glanced back, and the sunlight glinted on something on the saloon balcony.

What was that?

The barrel of a rifle reflected the light.

It was aimed directly at Nick.

"Nick!" she screamed. "Look out!"

Nick whirled her direction. She threw her arm out and pointed at the balcony.

It was only when she looked again that she realized the shooter's face was directed at her. His sharp gaze cut through the distance.

In a blink, his gun barrel pivoted, redirecting toward her.

Nick shouted something, the words not registering.

Run! The word pulsed in her head.

But she couldn't seem to make her feet move. Until the crack of the rifle split the air.

Time slowed as Nick watched the gunman aim his gun toward Elsie and fire.

No!

Nick sprang into motion, but the inches of snow slowed his steps.

"Elsie! Run!"

She'd already disappeared between two buildings by the time he got the words out. He hadn't seen. Had she fallen? Been shot?

"Nick, get down," Ed shouted from behind him.

Ed was right.

There was an entire block between him and the spot Elsie had disappeared. The streets were empty, and Nick made an easy target out in the open like this. He couldn't help Elsie if he was dead.

Head pounding, he ducked into the alley.

Bullets ricocheted off the walls behind him, not two feet away. A volley of shots answered.

Ed? Nick hadn't seen where his brother might've taken cover.

Pain flamed down his arm from the stitches in his shoulder.

He had one thought. Get to Elsie.

He ran down the alley to the narrow passageway behind the businesses.

Please let her be okay.

That bullet had been meant for him. If Elsie hadn't called out, he would have been shot. Was she all right?

He turned the corner. Down at the end of the street, Elsie huddled next to the shop wall.

Relief blasted him as he ran toward her. "Elsie!"

Face pale, eyes wide and terrified, she looked up at him as he heaved. He didn't hesitate to pull her into his arms.

She folded against him, shaking. Her hands trembled as she gripped onto his coat.

He didn't want to let go but put a few inches between them to scan her black coat for any sign she'd been shot. "Are you hurt? Did he hit you?"

"I don't think so." A haunted look shadowed her eyes.

His eyes slid closed. *Thank You, Lord.*

They needed to find safety, but a swell of emotion paralyzed his legs. His hand came to cup her cheek. "What were you thinking? Calling out like that." He fired the words at her.

She flinched.

The Nick I knew would never speak so cruelly.

The words knocked the breath out of his lungs as the memory surfaced.

"I couldn't let him shoot you," she said, her voice choked with tears.

At her words, he blinked back to the present. He needed to get her to safety. Quickly.

He pressed a kiss to her forehead "Come on. Let's go."

Grabbing her hand, he pulled her through the snowy alley, Patch at their heels.

The safest place to go was the marshal's office. If Marshal O'Grady was in town, she'd have heard those shots. And Ed would look for them there.

He glanced back to check on Elsie, who still looked terrified. Was she all right?

Another memory rushed in. An image of Elsie with tears streaming down her face. Within the memory, he felt satisfaction that he'd hurt her.

He blinked rapidly, almost tripping on a snow-covered crate. The memory stuck.

A wave of dizziness hit him as darkness slipped over his vision, bringing another memory.

A living room full of overdone Christmas decorations. He heard himself say, *I guess we never really knew each other at all.*

"Nick?"

Elsie's voice sounded as if she were far away. He felt the tug of Patch pawing his leg.

A sharp pain pierced his brain, and he leaned his shoulder into the nearest wall.

You didn't really want to marry me. You were simply desperate.

Images of a hurt Elsie, a furious Elsie, swam through his mind.

I would've at least fought for you. Which is more than what you did for me.

She hadn't fought for him.

You can't just waltz back into my life and pretend it never happened.

A wave of resentment assaulted his senses as memories began to overlap one another.

"Nick! Are you hurt?" He felt her tuck herself into his side, pull his arm over her shoulder, just like she had at the doctor's office. "Lean on me. How much farther to the marshal?"

The marshal. Someone shooting at them. They had to go. He allowed her to lead him even as another wave of memories bombarded him.

He pressed his palm against his aching head.

You're the teacher.

Elsie was Calvin's teacher. She held the job that was supposed to be his. The lifelong dream that had started when his favorite teacher handed him a copy of *Around the World in Eighty Days* shattered in a moment. All because of Elsie.

He wasn't a teacher.

How could he love her and resent her all at the same time?

The next few moments were fragments of running, a terrified Elsie, his memories revealing the truth.

There were no more shots as he and Elsie rounded the

corner to the marshal's office and climbed onto the board-walk. He didn't hesitate to throw open the door, pulling Elsie inside. They'd made it. But a bitter feeling overtook him.

Elsie looked around at the empty space, walked to the desk. Picked up a sheet of paper.

Transporting Prisoner. Return Unknown.

A growl tightened his throat. Now what?

His head swam. His stomach churned.

He barely reached a trash barrel before he lost his dinner.

Elsie tried to come near, but he threw out his arm so she'd stay back.

She pushed a chair noisily across the floor to him. "Here, you need to rest."

He twitched away from her when she reached for the bandage at his head. "Leave me alone."

The words shoved out of his mouth. Uncontrolled. Raw.

Elsie flinched, watching him with a confused, hurt expression. It only banked his anger.

Patch's claws clicked on the floorboards as he came up to Nick.

Nick's shoulder throbbed with fiery pain. Had the stitches come undone while he'd been running?

Everything from their past, the fight on the boardwalk, the past three days all swirled together inside him.

Elsie's sweet kisses. Everything he'd wanted five years ago. Her betrayal. Getting kicked out of normal school.

All I wanted was to be noticed.

She'd told him more during those hours stranded in the blizzard than she'd revealed in the entirety of their months-long relationship. Imagining Elsie as that lost, hurting little girl moved him. But nothing could make up for what he'd suffered.

"How could you let me act a fool during the blizzard?" he demanded wearily.

He looked up to see Elsie trembling, the fingers of one hand pressed against her lips. He saw it in her eyes. She'd guessed his memory was back.

"You lied to me for three days straight." He couldn't contain his fury, and she flinched.

A sheen of moisture brightened the green within her hazel eyes. Her lips firmed. "The doctor told me to do anything I had to in order to keep you quiet and still. He said you could die if you went out into the storm with a head wound like yours."

The fire in her voice told him she was telling the truth. Or at least that she'd believed the doctor.

"Besides," she went on. "You were the one determined to keep me close."

Boot steps pounded on the boardwalk, and then Ed stomped through the door, looking harried. Relief crossed his expression when he saw Nick and Elsie.

Elsie turned her back, but not before Nick saw her hands swiping at her cheeks.

"Where's the marshal?" Ed seemed to sense the tension in the room, his eyes bouncing between Elsie and Nick. "Everyone all right?"

No one answered him. Ed strode to the desk, looked at the note. Muttered something low. "It was Quade doing the shooting. I saw him clearly before he ducked into the saloon."

Nick had only seen the shooter's profile, and from too far away to identify him. Elsie had been closer.

Realization prickled down his spine.

Nick looked at Elsie, who still stood with her back to him. "Did you see his face?"

She gave a curt nod, but didn't turn.

Fear rolled over Nick.

If she had been close enough to see Quade's face, he'd definitely seen hers. What would Quade do to silence her?

Ed sent Nick a grim look that said he'd had the same realization.

And it was Nick's fault Elsie was in danger. He couldn't stand to look at her, but it was his obligation to protect her. But he couldn't guard her and his heart at the same time. He needed space.

Ed went to the window. "It's not safe to stay here without the marshal or her deputies. Quade will be looking for us."

Nick pinched the bridge of his nose. The room was spinning again, and a sudden wave of exhaustion hit him.

"Could you help me get back to my rooms?"

Nick looked up, but Elsie's words were directed at Ed, who flicked a look at Nick.

"You can't go home, Elsie," Nick said. "You'd be far too easy to find there."

For a moment, the same terror hit that he'd felt when he'd thought the gunman had shot her.

"I'll go to Merritt's, then. Surely Jack can keep me safe enough."

It was a decent suggestion, but Ed was shaking his head. "You'll be safest at the McGraw spread with us," he said gently.

"No." Her voice quivered. "I can't—"

"We don't have a choice," Nick bit out. He pushed himself to stand, glad when the room only wobbled a little.

She still wouldn't look at him, but he said it anyway. "You just witnessed attempted murder, Elsie. You'll have to come with us."

She shook her head slightly.

"Quade tried to shoot me," Nick said. "And then you."

Ed had gone quiet, finally realizing things weren't right between Nick and Elsie. "He won't let this go," he said now.

Nick saw when the realization slumped her shoulders. Her life depended on returning to the ranch with them.

But how was he going to survive with her underfoot?

Ten

WITH THE SUN BEGINNING TO CAST dawn's pinkish light on the eastern horizon, Elsie realized she should have never let the McGraw men convince her to return to their family homestead.

After the dustup in the marshal's office, Ed had been the most calm and rational. It'd been his plan to lie low for a while, then sneak over to the livery and rent a sleigh.

Elsie had felt the bile of uncertainty as she and Rebekah had bundled into the sleigh in the dark of night. It had taken a low argument between the brothers and Nick's approach for her to realize he meant to ride in the sleigh with them.

Humiliation had poured over her like thick molasses when Nick had insisted Rebekah move so he wouldn't be next to Elsie.

Nick hadn't said a word to her since the marshal's office—had only driven the horses through hours of snowy terrain.

Ed was riding Surrey, Nick's horse, scouting ahead for danger. Rebekah had stopped speaking after several awkward attempts to begin a conversation. Elsie was left to stew in her thoughts.

Nick hated her. She'd known it was bound to happen. She'd hoped to be away from him when his memories returned. Nothing had prepared her for the hollowness inside.

Before the snowstorm, she'd been fine. Content at least. Those hours spent with the tender Nick had reignited the feelings she'd had for him years ago. It had been hard enough to move on from him the first time. How was she going to do so again?

The sleigh topped a hill, and a homestead came into view. Elsie took it all in as Ed circled his horse behind the sleigh.

The home was nestled into a snowy valley with a barn on the other side of an expansive yard. The original lodge had been built with logs, while the newer addition and upstairs were plank.

A glow emanated from the windows, inviting and warm.

Pesky tears sprang to Elsie's eyes. That invitation surely wasn't for her.

Nick drove the sleigh close to the house and stopped. He moved to help the women out of the sleigh. Ed's horse blew.

Now the sun was coming up, and Elsie couldn't seem to stop shivering after hours in the sleigh.

The door was flung open, and a man with Nick's tall

stature stepped out. The confused dip of his brow reminded Elsie of Papa Bear, ready to scold.

Thinking back to when Nick had talked about his brothers, she guessed this must be Drew.

Drew's eyes swept over Nick as he gingerly got out of the sleigh. His frown deepened. "What happened?"

Ed was pulling packages from the sleigh. "We've got a problem in town."

A tall, lanky kid with dark hair stepped out. He turned back inside and yelled, "Uncle Nick and Uncle Ed are back."

Rebekah brushed past him with a hello.

An adolescent girl burst outside followed by a younger girl, hair in braids, neither wearing a coat. The little one ran straight for Nick and wrapped her arms around his waist.

Nick winced and embraced the child with stiff movements. He probably ached everywhere. "Hello, munchkin. Don't get your socks all wet."

Drew and the teen boy moved to help unload the sleigh, talking with Ed in low voices.

A smaller woman with blonde hair peeked out the door. She had a shawl wrapped around her. Even so, Elsie could see she was in the family way. "Welcome home. You're just in time for breakfast."

"Who're you?" the littlest girl demanded of Elsie.

Every eye turned toward her. She felt like a new student joining the class for the first time at midterm.

"That's Elsie," Ed said when Elsie hesitated a moment too long.

There was a flurry of introductions made. Elsie was aware

of the raised eyebrows from Drew and Kaitlyn. Even more aware that Nick didn't look at her once.

Ed faced Drew. "We really need to talk."

Inside, everyone bustled around, all in sync, everyone with a job.

Once the littlest girl had taken Elsie's coat, Elsie stood out of the way, near the staircase. She spent the moments using the little memory trick she'd learned during her first weeks as a brand-new teacher, committing everyone's name to memory.

An exclamation from Drew, where he conversed in a tight circle with Ed and Nick, drew her attention.

Nick was staring at her, eyes lit with banked anger and something else she couldn't identify.

She tipped her chin up, holding his stare. She'd explained her side of things, why she'd helped him in the clinic. What more did he want from her?

Tillie ran up to her, breaking into the moment. "Are you going to be my new aunt?"

Elsie's mouth opened, but all that came out was a squeak. She cleared her throat, then tried again. "No."

Tillie's brow scrunched. "But I thought Uncle Nick was getting himself a wife."

The reminder was enough to steal the breath from Elsie's chest, but Jo, the eleven-year-old, called from the dining table, "That ain't your business, nosy-body. Come set the table!"

Tillie went to join her sister but sent a confused look over her shoulder. "She looks like a wife."

When Elsie glanced at Nick again, he was staring at the floor, a muscle in his cheek jumping.

This wouldn't do. Elsie was nothing to Nick, and they both knew it.

She was stuck here for the foreseeable future. There had to be a way to make the best of it.

She had moved past the dining table and peeked into the kitchen when the front door burst open again and another part of the family came inside, brushing new snow from their coats.

More introductions were made. Inscrutable Isaac. A U.S. marshal, she remembered.

Captivating Clare. His wife. Eli and Ben, two boys who flung themselves at David, spoke rapid-fire.

By the time Elsie had taken in the newcomers, the table had been loaded with food.

Elsie felt as useless as a knickknack in the corner. An echo of that old feeling of being in the way, from when she'd lived with the Granbys, swept over her.

It didn't take long for the family to find their places around the table, although Elsie hesitated behind an empty chair. Was she taking someone else's seat?

The other side of the table had one long bench instead of chairs. The three boys had taken one end and were tussling in a way that reminded Elsie of a pair of brothers in her classroom.

Jo came to the end of the bench, where only a few inches of space remained. "This is my seat," she muttered as she plopped down. The boys kept shoving, and Elsie watched as Jo was knocked off the end of the bench, falling on her rump.

The boys cackled and laughed.

Jo's face was flushed with hurt as she scrambled to her feet.

Elsie's chest clenched as the girl fled. How many times had the Granby boys picked on her like that? But Drew caught Jo as she moved to pass him, put his arm around her shoulders, leaned in to say something in her ear.

Jo brightened, and watching the poignant moment between father and daughter made Elsie ache so badly she had to look away.

Unfortunately, her gaze immediately clashed with Nick's. He knew that the tender moment between father and daughter had affected her. She could see it in his eyes.

And when he quickly looked away, a second wave of emptiness hit Elsie.

She hadn't had a father to encourage her, protect her. And she didn't have Nick.

She felt like she was fumbling through the motions as dapper David encouraged her to sit.

Nick sat kitty-corner from her across the table. She wouldn't look at him again. It hurt too much.

She bowed her head for the blessing, accepted the food passed her way.

Until David handed her another bowl. "This is Momma's special recipe. She makes the best baked beans in the county." He leaned over and whispered, "She puts bacon in them."

Elsie only hesitated a moment before she accepted the bowl.

She hated beans. Ever since the Granbys. Even now, she imagined their gritty texture stuck in the back of her throat.

But the McGraws had been kind enough to take her in. It would be rude—Elsie lifted a spoonful from the bowl, aiming for her plate.

"Elsie doesn't like beans," Nick snapped from across the table.

Drew raised one eyebrow from where he sat next to Nick. But David shrugged as if it wasn't a big deal, so she passed the beans on.

No one else paid any attention, but Elsie caught the way Nick was grinding his teeth. Was he mad at her? Because she'd been going to eat those beans rather than cause a stir?

"He's desperate." Isaac's intense statement to Drew distracted her. "If he's personally pulling the trigger and not hiding behind a hired gun, he's too far gone to be reasoned with."

Rebekah set down her water glass with a clunk. "After that debacle with the Barlow Gang, he's lost the respect of all the townspeople."

"He's been frequenting the saloon," Ed said.

"It's still our word against his," Drew said. He'd barely touched his food. "No one saw him shoot during that blizzard. And we're the only ones who know that was him on the balcony yesterday."

Isaac pierced Elsie with glittering green eyes. "Seems like you've got one more eyewitness. Schoolmarm, well-liked and respected. No one's gonna doubt—"

"No." The cold word from Nick brought silence to the entire table. He stared at his plate, a stubborn set to his jaw. "This is our fight."

"He knows she saw his face," Ed argued quietly. Even the kids had gone quiet, and Elsie saw their wide eyes in her peripheral vision.

"Isaac's right," Drew said in a convincing tone. "Elsie's testimony would only add to ours—"

"I said no," Nick snapped. His face was flushed, his eyes sparking as he looked from brother to brother. "She doesn't owe us anything."

She didn't. There was no way to make things right after what'd happened between them years ago.

But Nick had put his own life in danger protecting her.

And testifying was the right thing to do.

His protectiveness stirred her belly. Almost like he still cared.

Would things have been different if she'd been brave enough to stand up for him in teaching school?

Her choice back then had changed everything for him.

"I'll do it," she said before she could change her mind.

It was well past dark when Nick slipped out of the bunkhouse, closing the door on a snoring David and Eli.

His bunk was a breeding ground for unwanted thoughts, and the glow of the moon didn't help. Nor did it erase the feel of Elsie's kiss from two days ago, replaying in his mind. The memory was turning him inside out.

And he was angry at Isaac for asking her to testify. Angrier that she'd said yes.

He entered the house, silence greeting him, then started a pot of coffee, wincing when he accidentally clanked the stovetop.

He was aware—too aware—that the reason for his insomnia was asleep upstairs in the girls' room.

As the coffee boiled, Nick looked through the kitchen window over the sink, staring at the silver moon glowing off the white landscape. It seemed so peaceful he could almost believe they were safe.

But it was an illusion.

Just like the past four years disappearing from his memory had been an illusion.

It was as if, for a few days, his mind had created an alternate world where his hopes and dreams had come true.

And her kiss. His eyes slid closed, remembering.

It hadn't been like the kisses they'd shared years ago. This one had come from Elsie the woman. Gone was the innocent, naive Elsie. But who was this older version of the Elsie he'd known? He didn't know her. But some part of him wanted to.

Which was why he couldn't sleep.

The coffee boiled over with a hiss, and he roused himself back to the present.

He couldn't focus on her kiss. Yes, it had really happened, but so had their argument in school. Her words still rattled his core, spoken with such venom he could almost smell its vitriol.

It's not like you mattered that much anyway.

He ground his teeth together. Those words had hit their target and made him bleed, but they competed against the memories of her snuggled close to his side in the doctor's clinic. And of her saving his life.

The vulnerability in her eyes when he'd said he loved her—

Nick jerked himself to the shelf with tin mugs. Anything to keep his mind from going there.

The coffee steamed as he poured, warming his inner chill.

If only she hadn't agreed to testify against Quade. Why had she done that, anyway?

A need to protect her flared within his gut.

Ah, drat. How had he let her get under his skin? Again.

The kitchen door swung open, and Nick startled, his coffee almost sloshing over the rim of his cup.

Isaac slipped inside. He must've assigned himself first patrol. His hat was pulled down low to keep the wind out of his face.

He did a double take when he caught sight of Nick standing in front of the kitchen counter next to the window.

Isaac stepped close enough to whisk Nick's coffee mug out of his hand. "Shouldn't you be sleeping?"

Isaac hadn't missed a thing at dinner. Nick had shown too much. Having Elsie close was like a burr under his saddle. "I didn't make that coffee for you."

Isaac ignored him and sipped the coffee. Nick felt the scrutiny of his brother's direct gaze.

"So, are you going to tell me about Elsie?"

Nick rubbed his forehead to ease the persistent headache

he couldn't rid himself of. He leaned against the counter. Maybe he should forget the coffee.

"There was a time when I was lost over Clare, and you set me straight."

He should've known Isaac would push.

"How come none of us knew about Elsie?"

Nick had helped Isaac muddle through his feelings for Clare, but that didn't mean Nick needed the favor reciprocated. He didn't want to have feelings for Elsie.

Isaac put down the coffee and widened his stance, blocking Nick's escape to the door. "Is she the reason you left school?"

The pain, the unfairness of the situation, his failure, it all still rubbed that raw place as if it'd happened yesterday.

Weariness settled over Nick's body. Why couldn't he feel this tired when he lay in bed?

"I guess your silence is all the yes I need."

Nick ran a hand down his face. Isaac wasn't going to let this go. "Elsie and I met in normal school. And I—"

He remembered the flutter in his stomach the first time he'd made her laugh. How his pulse had skipped as they'd decorated the school Christmas tree. Their first kiss . . .

But none of it had mattered in the end.

"I've never met anyone I could connect with on such an intellectual level. I wanted to marry her. Find a post where we'd teach together."

Isaac nudged the mug of coffee toward Nick. "What happened?"

Nick didn't want it anymore. Not with the way his stomach was churning. He sighed. "The dean's son was infatuated with Elsie. He warned me to back off. I told him no."

Isaac shrugged. "Sounds fair."

The hollowness in Nick's gut grew. What would his brother say about what he had to reveal next? "Shortly after my last term started, I was called into the dean's office. They claimed to have a witness who saw me stealing a test. When the dean searched my room, he found the test. I was expelled on the spot for cheating."

He'd never forget the fire flashing through his veins at seeing the papers in Dean Sullivan's hand. Knowing he'd been framed and was powerless to defend himself.

Pa had always said that carrying the McGraw name meant integrity. And he had brought shame to the family.

He'd thrown himself into work on the ranch, trying to forget his dream of teaching. And Elsie.

Isaac stood motionless, his face unreadable.

Nick looked at the floor. "I know it was the dean's son who framed me. But no one believed me."

Isaac moved to lean into the counter next to Nick. "So how does Elsie play into this? She didn't believe your side of the story?"

Nick could barely get the words out. "The night that the witness claimed he saw me coming out of the office, I was with Elsie. Alone."

Issac expelled a quiet "Oh."

That was the crux of it. "Nothing improper happened. We just talked. I might've stolen a kiss or two. We would meet sometimes at this big oak behind the dormitories."

Those stolen moments had been so precious.

"She was your alibi," Isaac deduced.

Nick rubbed the back of his neck. "But if she'd admitted to it—"

"She'd have been labeled promiscuous and expelled."

Nick hadn't understood until later what she would've risked, would have lost, by such an admission. He'd been hurt, had felt betrayed by Elsie, the dean, the system itself.

He'd wanted her to choose him. Why hadn't he been enough?

He turned to pace, shoving his hand through his hair. "I was so angry with her. All I ever wanted was to be a teacher, and because she refused to stick up for me, I was expelled."

But even as the words left his mouth, he heard the selfishness in them.

"You put her in a difficult spot."

It'd taken Isaac seconds to understand what it had taken Nick years to admit.

More pieces fell into place as what she'd told him about her childhood resurfaced in his memory.

She'd been unwanted. Abandoned. Her desperation to please her adoptive parents made more sense now.

And Nick had walked away from her.

Shame and guilt clawed at his gut.

Isaac scratched the stubble along his jaw. "Seems to me she's sticking up for you now."

Nick couldn't answer him, not with the way his emotions were knotted.

Isaac stared out the window like Nick had earlier. "You told me I deserved a second chance. Maybe the two of you deserve another chance?"

Nick was already shaking his head. What was done was done. He couldn't open his heart to Elsie again.

Isaac went on, "And why don't you deserve to go back to school?"

Why not go back to school?

Nick cleared his throat. "I have responsibilities here. And Pa warned me to not chase after rainbows."

He could still see the disappointed expression on Pa's face every time Pa had found him reading instead of tossing hay bales or finishing another ranch chore.

Isaac shook his head. "You think Pa never had to tell Drew to get his head out of the clouds? You know how he was horse crazy. Or that he didn't warn me off being marshal? Pa had his own way of thinking. Doesn't mean it was right for me. Or for you."

Silence stretched between them.

Nick appreciated Isaac's advice, but he was too old for normal school now. Most people there were fresh-faced kids.

Isaac thumped Nick's back. "Try and get some sleep, little brother. This thing with Quade ain't over."

Nick watched Isaac leave.

For the first time, Nick wanted to forgive Elsie. Maybe already had. But that didn't mean there was a future for them.

As Nick trudged back to the bunk house, the echo of second chances rang in his ears.

The difference between Isaac's second chance and one for Nick was the timeline. Forgiveness was one thing, but going back in time . . . impossible.

Besides, Elsie had been so passionate about teaching, she wouldn't let anything stand between her and her dream.

Including Nick. She'd never choose him over being a teacher.

Eleven

MORNING CAME, AND THE SLEEPLESS night had left Nick sluggish and hungry.

He crossed the threshold to the kitchen, then froze at the sight of Elsie standing at the counter and rolling out biscuit dough. Alone.

Where was everyone else? He blinked hard to make sure he wasn't still dreaming.

Last night, he'd fallen into a restless sleep, thoughts of forgiveness and second chances spiraling through his head.

Now, watching Elsie fidget with the roller in her hands, he waited for the sharpness of his anger to return. But it didn't.

He just felt resigned.

"Good morning." The quiver of Elsie's smile said she wasn't sure he'd return the greeting.

Last night's talk with Isaac had put things into perspective, but where did that leave Nick? Was being friends even an option?

He slid his hands into his pockets, his shoulder paining. "Morning."

Her attention flitted about the kitchen as she kept rolling the dough.

Rubbing his pulsing shoulder, he tore his eyes away and scanned the room. The kitchen appeared extra clean. She'd obviously been busy this morning. How long had she been up?

Nick made for the coffeepot on the stove, even though it put him near Elsie. But if they were to continue as friends, he could be close long enough to get coffee.

As he poured, he could smell the lavender soap she'd used to wash up competing with the coffee's earthy aroma. It did strange things to his stomach.

When he passed by, her hand cutting away the dough stuttered.

The early morning hush over the house resounded around them. She didn't look at him. It reminded him of those first hours at the clinic. Just the two of them.

She'd avoided his gaze then too, but at least now, Nick understood why.

He cleared his throat. "Did you, ah, sleep well?"

She kept her focus on her hand as she cut circles in the dough. "As well as I could stuck between Jo and Tillie. Jo wasn't so bad, but Tillie, she—"

"Holds an entire conversation in her sleep. Yep." Nick smirked as he took a sip.

She blinked up at him. For a moment, her nose wrinkled.

Then she scooted around him to collect the skillet next to the cookstove. "I couldn't go back to sleep, so I came down here to see how I could help."

By preparing his family a meal. "No one expects you to do all of this."

The skillet clanged as she pulled it from under the counter and onto the stove. "It's the least I can do."

She began to slice the bacon. He knew how stubborn she could be and left her to it when he heard the murmur of his brothers' voices from the dining room. Without a glance toward Elsie, he made his escape.

Around the table, his brothers leaned toward each other, speaking in low tones. Ed's head shot up as Nick entered, his words trailing off. All three went suspiciously silent.

Ed spun a coffee mug in his hand, and Drew took a sip from his.

"What's going on?"

The momentary silence was stifling.

Ed and Drew glanced at each other sideways. Isaac leaned back in his chair and crossed his arms. "Nick's got the most strategic mind out of all of us." He kicked out an empty chair. "Have a seat. What do you think Quade will do next?"

Nick had been so caught up in his feelings for Elsie that he hadn't given Quade a thought since they'd left town.

He sat, not much liking that his brothers hadn't waited on him.

Isaac tipped his head toward Ed. "Ed thinks Quade will wait for one of us to come into town and ambush us again, but I think he'll hole up at his main house."

Nick set his coffee on the table. "We know Quade lost most of his hired hands when everything went down with the Barlow Gang. And Isabella is straitlaced. He wouldn't go back to the main house, not if she's there asking questions."

"So he would stay in town," Ed said.

Nick thought for a minute. "Not unless he's acting alone, which he likely isn't. He's probably hired guns since Elsie saw him shooting at us. I bet he barricaded himself in one of his smaller homesteads."

Isaac looked grim. "We don't have enough deputies to search all of Quade's holdings. With just us, it'd take days."

Nick pointed to the star pinned to Isaac's vest. "Can't you deputize more men? Just until he's captured. Fogelson would help. Charlie Hastings too."

A dangerous gleam shone in Isaac's eyes. "I sure can."

Ed plunked his coffee mug down on the table. "Good. We should get going."

The other brothers started to stand.

Nick guzzled the rest of his coffee and stood along with them.

The brothers stilled, all of them refusing to look Nick in the eye. When Isaac finally did look his way, regret shadowed his face.

Oh. Nick wasn't invited. A sick feeling rolled in his stomach.

Drew reached over and put a hand on Nick's shoulder. "We need you here."

Sure they did. They just didn't want Nick to slow them down.

"Someone has to watch over our families," Isaac added.

Nick shrugged away from Drew's hand. "They don't need me here. Clare is a sharpshooter."

Ed, the conflict avoider, was already out the door.

Drew scratched his eyebrow. "You're injured, Nick. The one Quade would target because you're—"

"Weak?"

Isaac's stare hardened. "Hurt."

"I'm healed enough to ride." The dull ache in his head belied the words.

How many times had he, the youngest, watched his brothers ride out without him?

Drew reached for his coat on the peg. "Nick—"

Nick gave in with bad grace. "I get it. I'll stay behind."

Isaac looked like he wanted to say something.

Nick didn't need his brother's pity. "I'll go saddle up your horses."

He spun to make his exit, but as he did, a shadow moved away from the kitchen doorway.

Fantastic. How long had Elsie been listening?

He stomped though the kitchen, avoiding eye contact with Elsie, who stood at the stove.

He'd almost reached the back door when Elsie murmured, "The gravy is ready. Do you want—"

"Later," he growled as embarrassment heated his cheeks. Even the morning chill couldn't cool his temper.

With pent-up energy flowing into his arms, he shoved the barn door open. Searing pain permeated his shoulder all the way down to his hand.

He bit his lip to stifle a pained holler.

Bracing his shoulder with his other hand, he crumpled into the support beam, inhaling deeply.

If he couldn't handle opening the barn door, what made him think he could help round up Quade? He must be a fool. He *was* the weakest. He hated the thought.

When the pain subsided to a dull anguish, he saddled his brothers' horses and led them to the front of the house.

Drew and Kaitlyn stood on the porch, hands entwined. He whispered something to her, his brow tight as he rested a hand on her belly. He bent and kissed her, gentle and slow.

Nick could see Ed and Rebekah through the front window, embracing. Isaac and Clare were barely visible around the corner of the house, saying a private goodbye.

All three of Nick's brother had found their perfect matches, had families to fight for. Another way they'd left him behind.

He'd thought to try again—that's why he'd asked Merritt to help him find someone. But thinking about courting someone who wasn't Elsie put a bitter taste in his mouth. Was he kidding himself? Was he destined to be alone?

Nick averted his gaze but caught Elsie watching through the front window. Their stares collided, and his heart thumped.

She let the curtain drop back into place.

A hand fell on Nick's shoulder, and he startled.

Isaac took his horse's reins from Nick's hand, but before he stepped away, Isaac's eyes flitted to the window, then back to Nick.

"Second chances, little brother."

Then Isaac mounted and motioned for the brothers to follow him.

They took off at a canter down to the road, leaving Nick standing by himself in their wake.

Elsie dried the final dish and stacked it on top of the other clean ones on the counter.

Nick was pushing himself too hard. If he didn't come in from the barn soon, he might hurt his shoulder. Or head.

Elsie looked out the window, like she had probably a hundred times within the last hour. She considered going down to the barn to check on him. Knew he would not welcome it, even if he'd smiled at her earlier.

His brothers had been gone for two hours, and Nick hadn't been inside since. He'd skipped breakfast.

The house had grown quiet. Clare and Eli had returned to Isaac's cabin to gather a few things plus additional ammunition. For the worst-case scenario, according to Clare.

Just the thought of worst-case frightened Elsie.

Kaitlyn had looked tired, so Rebekah had sent her upstairs to rest while she helped occupy the kids in the living room.

Which left Elsie to clean up breakfast. And worry about Nick.

With a sharp sigh, she started to turn away from the window but froze. Nick had finally emerged from the barn, carrying a load of firewood.

Surely he hadn't chopped it.

Even from a distance, she could see the stiffness in his gait.

He was upset about being left behind. She knew that from what she'd accidentally overheard earlier this morning.

And she didn't know how to make it better.

Wood clattered against the outside kitchen wall as he stacked it.

She held her breath, waiting for him to come inside.

And waiting.

Something must be wrong.

With a huff, she moved to the door before she could change her mind.

Cold air sliced through her dress as she marched across the back porch to where he stood with one arm against the wall next to the woodpile.

He knew she was there. She could tell by the way his shoulders went even more tense. But he didn't turn to face her. Or say anything.

Elsie rubbed her arms, partly to stave off the wind and partly to keep herself from reaching for him.

She blinked. "Would you come in already?"

He slowly turned his head and eyed her.

The greenish hue underneath the flush on his cheeks made her pulse fly.

"Last night, you were willing to eat the beans you hate to keep from hurting Kaitlyn's feelings. But you've got no compunction in bossing me around."

His almost teasing words were such a surprise that it took her a moment to respond. "I guess you're just special."

He pushed against the wall to straighten, but his balance was off, and he wobbled.

She was already reaching for him before she thought better of it and let her arms drop back to her sides.

He stared at her hands, unmoving. "I'm fine."

No, he wasn't. "You've hurt your head."

He ignored that, wincing as he pushed away from the wall again and brushed by her.

Elsie shifted on her feet before she followed him in and closed the door, still shivering.

Nick slid off his coat, his movements stiff, then hung it on a peg before crossing over to the sink. He primed the pump to wash his hands.

Elsie couldn't ignore the rawness of his expression. Something inside called her to ease his pain. "You need to sit before you fall over." She pulled out a chair from the small table in the corner. "You missed breakfast, but I'll make you something to eat."

With pressed lips, he looked at her, then the chair, wiping his hands slowly on a towel.

Elsie swallowed. "Please."

He tossed the towel onto the counter. "Only if you quit bossing me around."

Nick was the only one who'd ever accused her of being bossy. The callback to how they'd once been pricked her heart. She moved to the larder to pull out the leftover biscuits from breakfast as he gingerly moved to the chair.

Nick stretched his legs out in front of him. She was conscious of the way he watched her. Gone was his anger from yesterday. He seemed almost uncertain.

She brought the plate over and set it down in front of him. "Nick, I know it's none of my business, but your brothers wanted you along. I know it. Your injury—"

He bristled. "I know that, Elsie. When a single load of firewood makes me feel like heaving, I know that I would've slowed them down."

He sounded so angry. How could he be angry at himself for having been shot?

He kept his head bowed over his plate, fingers playing with one of the biscuits.

"I can't let my family down again." His voice was soft, as if he hadn't meant to speak out loud. He smoothed his thumb along the cup, a faraway look on his face.

She sat in the chair across from him, avoiding his eyes. "You aren't letting your family down."

He folded his arms and braced them against the table. "I did when I chose to study over helping my dad one time. He ended up . . ."

His eyes closed, and Elsie's breath caught in her lungs. "Ended up what?"

His gaze flicked to her and then away again. He was silent for so long that she thought he wouldn't answer. And then words seemed to pour out of him.

"Back when I was studying for my entrance exam for normal school, my dad told me to move my green broke colt to the barn from the corral. I lost track of time studying."

"That's easy to do," Elsie murmured

He ran a hand down his face. "I was in the house and heard a commotion outside. Pa had tried to move my colt himself. It'd spooked and tossed my dad into the fence, stomped on his leg."

Before she could stop herself, Elsie reached out and laid her hand on Nick's arm. His muscle twitched beneath her hand, but he didn't push her away.

His throat bobbed as he swallowed. "His leg never healed properly. If I'd done what I was told, it never would've happened."

She hadn't known he bore this guilt. "Nick, it was an accident."

"A year later, he died." He rubbed his chest, as if his heart ached. "I was told his leg had some sort of infection that eventually killed him. Because of me chasing my dream, my dad died."

He moved his hand to rest on hers, its warmth rendering her speechless.

"My mom encouraged me to return to school, so I did all I could for the sake of proving my dad didn't die in vain, but then . . ."

Then.

A stone dropped in Elsie's gut. No wonder he'd been so angry. So hurt.

Had she been the selfish one? Not understanding the guilt he carried?

He looked up at her, the shame in his expression making her ache. "My priorities were all mixed up. I can't let anything distract me from my responsibilities."

Was that how he saw himself? How he thought his brothers saw him? She couldn't stand the thought.

"Your family doesn't need another warrior. What they need is you. Your brothers need you to help them."

Nick's expression was unreadable. "They need another gun at their backs. Not someone to sit at home."

How could she explain so he'd understand? "You've a way of seeing what no one else sees. You see Quade's next move. You see a different approach. You see a kid who needs a kind word." She swallowed. "You saw a frightened girl on her first day of teaching school and made her feel included. Like she belonged."

His eyes held hers, and her heart pattered in her chest.

Elsie's throat clenched so tight, she had to force out "You noticed me."

He drew away, leaving her to put her hand in her lap. A muscle in his jaw ticked. "How could anyone not notice you?"

Heat gathered behind her eyes. Maybe he'd noticed her then, but after, he'd forgotten all about her.

He simply stared.

And the kitchen door swung open.

"Is it time for lunch? I'm starving." Jo headed straight for the larder as if she hadn't even noticed Nick and Elsie sitting there.

Elsie stood, her movements stiff. "Not quite."

Awareness pricked as Nick's eyes followed her when she crossed to help Jo. Maybe the interruption was for the best.

They both knew there was no future together, not for the two of them. It was no use focusing on the past.

She needed to make it through the next few days with her heart intact.

Twelve

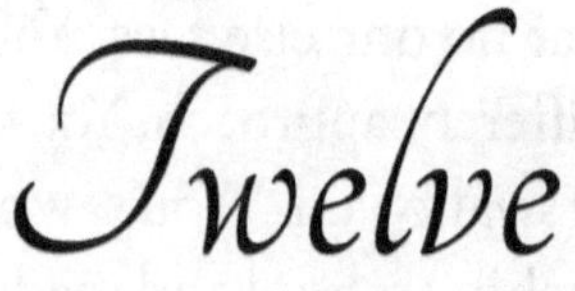

ELSIE HAD NEVER MANAGED A CLASS-
room like this.

"Gimme!" Ben cried.

"I won it fair and square!" Tillie stuck out her tongue at him.

Their game of marbles had gone on for too long. Elsie had sat down to supervise a while ago, and now her left foot was asleep.

Across the living room, Eli and Jo lay on their stomachs with a checkerboard between them. Jo snatched up a checker with a cackle, and Eli cried, "Hey, give that back or I'll slug you."

"There will be no slugging!" Elsie called out.

Eli pulled a face but ducked back to the game momentarily.

It had been a day and a half since the men left on their mission, and tempers were short.

Between the sense of possible danger and the soft snow that had been falling since last night, the kids had been cooped up in the house for too long.

Even Elsie's real students got breaks to run around outside and release pent-up energy.

Something was on the brink, and the entire household could feel it.

Ben carefully angled his blue shooter marble toward the only two remaining marbles on the other side of the circle. Tillie had lost interest, balancing her shooter on her upper lip.

Footsteps overhead were a reminder that Rebekah had gone up to check on Kaitlyn, who'd been in bed all morning. Elsie didn't know much about pregnancy, but Rebekah had helped her prepare breakfast with a worried frown.

Clare and David had gone to the barn for chores. Was Nick out there?

She'd barely seen Nick since the emotional conversation yesterday morning. He'd walked circles around the property, scouting for danger. Spent the rest of the time in the barn or bunkhouse. Maybe he'd come to the same conclusion she had after their talk.

She needed to keep her distance. Otherwise she risked opening her heart to him again.

Ben tossed his arms in the air. "I win again!"

Tillie whined. "I'm bored. Let's play Sculptor again."

Ben tossed the marbles, and they bounced noisily across the floor. "No way. We played that all morning."

One of the flying marbles pinged over the checkerboard, and Eli made a noise of outrage.

Elsie stood, using the sofa for balance when blood flow returned to her tingling foot. "Why don't we—"

A loud thump on the porch interrupted her, and the kids went quiet.

What was that?

The door swung open, and Nick blew in with a light swirl of snow. David was on his heels, and Patch followed last.

Tillie and Ben ran to his side with a string of questions before he could toe his boots off.

"What took you so long?"

"Can you take me outside?"

"How come David got to go?"

"Where's Clare?"

Nick smiled as he cued Patch to lie down on a blanket by the door and took off his gloves. "Clare's in the barn still."

Jo followed Nick as he moved toward the window to peer out. "Uncle Nick, I'm going to go crazy if I have to stay inside with all them."

Tillie propped her hands on her hips. "That's not nice."

"Let me grab a cup of coffee and warm up, you hooligans."

Elsie made a beeline for the kitchen. "I'll pour."

She met Nick at the stove. The grim set of his mouth was not reassuring.

"Thanks," he murmured when she pressed the warm cup into his chilled hands. He glanced over his shoulder. There was movement and voices through the doorway, but the kids had stayed put. For now.

"My brothers should've checked in by now," he said in a low voice.

She saw the concern in his expression. "I'm praying for them."

Something softened in his eyes until he seemed to realize himself and shake off his expression.

"Kaitlyn's been under the weather," she said quickly, not wanting this moment with him to end. "Rebekah is upstairs with her."

His forehead wrinkled. "They left you to watch all the kids?"

He seemed frustrated on her behalf.

It made her warm inside, even though she didn't expect him to be protective.

"I have four times as many students in my class," she said. And then regretted it when shadows darkened his eyes.

There was a crash from the front room, and they both turned in that direction.

"They're becoming a bit stir-crazy," she said.

"Everyone's worried," he said absently. "David and I had an idea that might help."

She trailed him back to the living room, where he clapped his hands once. Ben and Eli were tussling on the floor while Jo righted the coat rack.

"Who wants to decorate for Christmas?" Nick asked.

Elsie blinked. This was his idea?

The kids cheered. David went out the front door and quickly backed inside with a fir tree that was taller than he was in his arms.

Jo shot toward the kitchen door. "Can I pop the popcorn?"

"Hold up," Nick called to her. "Wait for an adult to help."

He moved to help David wrestle the tree into place while Tillie danced in circles.

Ben and Eli stood back watching. This was the quietest they'd been all day.

Elsie moved closer to Nick. "Are you sure about this? What about—" *Your brothers.*

He seemed to understand what she'd left unsaid. Would Drew, Ed, and Isaac be upset if they weren't included in this family tradition?

The corner of Nick's mouth lifted. "It'll be all right."

Ben stared at the tree. "What do we put on it?"

Kaitlyn had given Elsie a crash course on the family dynamics last night. She knew Ben and Eli were Clare's nephews and that they'd moved into the McGraw family weeks ago. The boys' parents were both gone.

She slipped her arm around Ben's shoulders. "What did your ma and pa put on your tree?"

Ben hesitated, and Eli was suspiciously silent. Tillie spoke up. "Eli and Ben never had Christmas before."

"So what?" Eli said with a tilt of his chin.

She saw the uncertainty in Ben's face.

What must their life have been like to never have celebrated something like Christmas?

Elsie's pa hadn't celebrated Christmas either after her mother died. At least, if he had, she didn't remember it.

After the Westons had taken her in, Darcy had gone out of her way to make Christmas special. But Elsie had always known her place with them wasn't guaranteed. Even at Christmas.

New purpose stirred excitement within Elsie. She looked

down at Ben, including Eli in her statement too. "Well, it's my first Christmas with the McGraws too. We can learn about McGraw traditions."

Ben brightened.

"Come help me stabilize the tree, Eli?" Nick's voice was muffled beneath the branches.

It wasn't long before everyone was busy. Clare had returned from the barn and was helping Jo pop heaps of corn. It kept mysteriously disappearing from the table where Jo, Eli, and Ben strung it with needles and thread.

Nick had brought in a crate of dried cornhusks to make ornaments, and the cornhusks were now soaking in a large metal bowl at the end of the table. Tillie flitted around the room, unable to contain her excitement.

"Can you help me tie a knot?" Ben asked. Elsie obliged.

Nick stepped back from the fireplace, his eyes scanning the progress. "That looks good, David. I like the pine bough on the mantel."

At Nick's words, Elsie glanced across the room, and their gazes collided. She quickly looked down to where she was showing Tillie how to fold a wet cornhusk into a star.

"Remember last Christmas, Jo?" David asked.

Jo held up her hands in surrender, the needle she was threading popcorn with still between her thumb and index finger. "I didn't know the barn cat would tip the tree over."

Tillie started to laugh, the husk unfolding in her hand. "That was funny."

David shook his head. "Pa was so mad."

Tillie scrunched her nose up. "Pa doesn't get so mad now

that he'n Kaitlyn are married," she proclaimed. She looked innocently up at Elsie. "Are you ever gonna get married?"

This time Elsie couldn't chance catching Nick's gaze. She kept her eyes on the cornhusk, guiding Tillie's fingers where they needed to go. "I don't know."

Why was it Nick was her first thought at the girl's innocent question? Arnold was the more likely candidate. Arnold, who she needed to write a return letter to.

Rebekah cleared her throat as she carried a bowl of freshly popped popcorn over to the table. "I remember when I was a kid, I loved helping my aunt make the best peppermint candy. We even put some on our tree."

Ben's eyes widened. "Can we do that?"

"Nope," Jo inserted. "David would eat it all."

"I would not."

"I might," Eli said.

A laugh burst out of Elsie.

She wrung out a soaking cornhusk and handed it to Tillie. Water droplets flew everywhere in the girl's exuberance. Elsie stilled Tillie's hands with a gentle touch. "I remember one of my first Christmases with the Westons. I missed my pa so much."

That Christmas, she'd sat by the window, hoping her father would finally come. He never had.

She cleared the emotion from her throat and wrung out another cornhusk for herself. "It was the first time I met Merritt. She'd come home with my sister Darcy for the break. Darcy must have noticed I was lonely, because she pulled me over to where she and Merritt had started making cornhusk dolls. Before long, they had me laughing and feeling at home."

Tillie made the next fold Elsie showed her. "How come you're not with your family now?"

It was a loaded question. All those expectations, waiting for her under the Westons' roof. "My sister is all grown up"—Elsie gave the girl the easier answer—"with a husband of her own. Christmas isn't the same without her."

It grew quiet around the table. Elsie kept her focus on the next cornhusk, those old feelings pressing in.

"Sometimes you need new traditions, Tillie." Nick's voice brought Elsie's head up. She hadn't noticed that he and David had joined them at the table, both trying to make a star.

Tillie nudged Elsie for the next step, but Elsie couldn't look away from Nick. His eyes were warm and compassionate, and she remembered what she'd told him in the doctor's clinic. Those broken pieces she'd always kept to herself. He knew now.

Here, in a crowded room, he saw the real her.

And the way he was looking at her—as if he were proud of her—rekindled all those old feelings.

She forced her eyes to the cornhusk when Tillie nudged her again.

"*The loss that brought us pain, That loss but made us love thee more.*" His voice was low as the kids chattered around them.

Tennyson.

Their game.

"*Ever gentle, and so gracious with all his learning.*"

Their eyes caught and held. A tiny, chagrined smile tugged at the corner of his mouth. He only looked away when Eli asked a question.

Elsie was left holding her breath.

She didn't know what to do with this Nick. He seemed to be extending an olive branch, offering his friendship. But every interaction reminded her of what they'd once had.

The room was suddenly stuffy, and she dropped the cornhusk and hurried into the kitchen. She needed space.

The aroma of freshly baked cookies washed over her as she leaned against the doorframe.

Rebekah glanced over from where she was rolling dough for more cookies. "Oh, good! Elsie, do you mind pulling out the tray in the oven?"

"Of course."

Happy for the distraction, Elsie picked up potholders.

"I can't help but observe, Nick seems more settled when he's with you," Rebekah said.

Elsie slid the pan from the oven, trying to hide her shaking hands. She didn't respond.

Rebekah placed the freshly cut cookies onto another pan. "Ed and I had a misunderstanding once. Before we were married. Back then, I'd just as soon snap at him than look at him. Now I realize we were meant to be together from the beginning."

Elsie's heart pinched. Why was Rebekah telling her this?

Rebekah picked up the pan with the fresh dough and held it out for Elsie to put in the oven. As Elsie took the tray, Rebekah held on as well, her expression adamant.

"Sometimes, if given a chance, beauty can come from ashes."

Elsie didn't move, even as Rebekah released the tray.

Beauty from ashes?

Nick's words in the marshal's office resounded in her head. *After this, we are nothing to each other.*

No, it was too late for them.

His poem had been an olive branch, but their future held nothing more than friendship.

Another six hours had passed. Almost thirty-six since Nick's brothers had left. Too long without anyone riding back to check in.

Nick stood at the parlor window as dusk painted the horizon dark purple, his eyes scanning for any movement.

The stillness rattled him. Something was coming, but he couldn't see it.

The house was decorated ceiling to floorboard. It should've felt festive, but the kids were picking up on the tension from the adults and growing restless again. They sat gathered at the long dining table after supper had been cleared.

The women had gone into the kitchen for cleanup. Pans and dishes clanked. He saw in the window's reflection when Elsie emerged from the kitchen and joined Tillie.

He'd go out and track his brothers down if he thought it would help. Though, with his head still aching off and on, he'd likely be more hindrance than help.

Christmas isn't the same without her.

Elsie's words from earlier kept running through his head. Elsie had worked miracles with the kids—keeping them busy with crafts and games, noticing Ben's and Eli's hesitancy and comforting them. She'd jumped in whole-heartedly.

She had so much love to give. But she'd told Rebekah she'd be spending Christmas alone.

It didn't make a lick of sense. Elsie took care of everyone else. But who took care of Elsie?

"I did not!" Eli cried. The punch he gave David, though they were sitting side by side on the bench, had some force to it.

Nick turned from the window, ready to intervene.

"Tillie just had a wonderful idea," Elsie interrupted. "Why don't we sing some Christmas carols?"

The words immediately threw him into a memory of their time at school—a night when a group had decided to go caroling.

Walking from house to house, he'd slowly maneuvered his way next to her in the crowd of carolers, allowing his shoulder to "accidentally" brush up against her. Once, she'd tried to teach him the tune, but his efforts had only made them both laugh until their sides ached.

Toward the end of the evening, an older couple had invited the carolers in for wassail. The fireplace had illuminated the room and his pulse had raced at the way the candlelight reflected across her face.

They'd stood next to the tree, out of sight of the other carolers, cups of wassail in their hand, talking about their hopes, their dreams, until he couldn't help but gently tug Elsie behind the Christmas tree when no one was looking.

He'd leaned down and brushed his lips across hers.

"Merry Christmas, El-Belle."

He'd never forget the way she'd smiled back, her heart in her eyes. "Merry Christmas, Mr. McGraw."

Had it been the enchanting night, or was it Elsie who created the magic?

David groaned, the sound bringing Nick back to the present. "Singing?"

Tillie ignored him and pulled Elsie to stand next to the tree, now crammed with dried apples, popcorn garland, and an array of cornhusk ornaments. "Let's sing 'Angels We Have Heard on High.'"

Jo wandered over more slowly. "You just like singing the gloria part at the top of your lungs. Let's sing 'We Three Kings.'"

Elsie laughed, and its ring echoed in the recesses of Nick's heart. "We can sing them all," she said.

"Until bedtime," Kaitlyn added as Nick's three sisters-in-law joined them. She lowered herself into a chair by the fireplace.

Nick pointed to the door. "It's time I make my rounds."

Rebekah chuckled. Everyone knew he couldn't carry a tune in a bucket.

But he got caught in Elsie's gaze before his feet moved an inch. "We need your voice. You're our only baritone."

She remembered. He saw it in her eyes, in the bittersweet smile.

Tillie slid her small hand into his, breaking the moment. "Please, Uncle Nick. Sing with us."

Elsie's words echoed in his head. *Your family needs more than a warrior.* Maybe, in this moment, swallowing his pride and singing was what they needed.

He heaved a sigh and swung Tillie up in his good arm. She squealed.

"Only if you promise to help me sing on pitch."

He sat in a chair facing the window, Tillie in his lap, as Elsie broke into a rendition of "Angels We Have Heard on High."

Elsie's voice rang out above the others, her soprano floating effortlessly. It reached out and nearly choked Nick. So beautiful.

But when they arrived at the chorus, Tillie lifted her chin and shouted the gloria with such gusto that the three boys started to snicker.

She responded by closing her eyes and singing loud enough to burst Nick's eardrum.

A laugh bubbled up from Nick's gut. No sense in letting Tillie have all the fun. So he joined her.

Eli wrapped his arms around his torso, laughing until he fell over on the floor. "Uncle Nick, please stop."

Nick glanced over at Elsie.

Another woman might have been annoyed at his silly antics, but not Elsie. She rolled her eyes at him, but she was smiling. The same way she had that night long ago.

The song ended with laughter bouncing around the room.

"Sing 'God Rest Ye Merry, Gentlemen,'" Jo said. "It's Ma's favorite."

"It's only Ma's favorite if Uncle Nick doesn't sing," David declared.

Nick put his hand onto his chest. "Why wouldn't you want me to sing?"

Ben leaned over the arm of Nick's chair. "Because you really stink at it."

Elsie pealed with laughter.

Nick pulled a face. "I happen to be a wonderful actor—"

"Acting ain't the same as singing," Eli called out.

Jo doubled over with giggles.

Nick's gaze found Elsie next to the tree, watching him. When his eyes met hers, she didn't look away. Only stared at him with an openness that made his heart soar.

With a shy smile, she started to sing. "God rest ye merry, gentlemen, let nothing you dismay . . ."

Oh, her voice sent a shiver up Nick's spine. The others joined in the carol, but Nick couldn't force his voice to work.

How did she fit in so perfectly with his family? Almost like she was the missing piece no one knew they needed.

Joy flushed her cheeks as she took Ben's hands and began to dance around the room. Kaitlyn started clapping, and others followed suit.

"From God our heavenly Father a blessed angel came . . ."

The tempo picked up speed, his heart keeping the same rhythm. Elsie danced Ben around the room faster to keep up until she huffed between words. Her arms lifted into the air with an exuberant "Hey!" at the end before she plopped backward onto the settee.

Cheers echoed around the room.

"Again!" Tillie shouted.

Elsie's hand came to her chest. "Let me catch my breath first. How about a slow one?"

Kaitlyn lifted up the first verse of "O Come, All Ye Faithful," and one by one, the family joined her.

Except for Elsie. Her smile dipped, a faraway expression on her face as she looked out the window. Was she thinking about when he'd whistled the tune in the clinic, no matter how poorly, while they'd huddled together to stay warm?

Or maybe her thoughts had turned to her real father. Or their time at school.

Whichever it was, an expression of sorrow passed over her face, and Nick's breath hitched.

Really, they'd been so young in school. Both trying to make adult decisions without really seeing the whole picture.

The more he knew her, the more he understood. For the little girl who'd been abandoned, love had always been conditional. Something to earn.

Once, he had told her he would forget about her, but the truth was he'd never forgotten.

What was he doing? He couldn't fall for her again.

He tore his gaze away. When he did, he saw Clare watching him with raised eyebrows.

He was making a fool of himself all over again.

Tillie nudged Nick with her elbow. "Come on, Uncle Nick, sing with me."

They had moved into "O Holy Night" and were almost to the chorus. Nick inhaled, then belted out, "Fall on your knees! O hear the angel voices . . ."

Nick's voice cracked on the top note, and Patch bolted up from where he'd curled by the door, releasing a long howl that overpowered every other voice in the room.

Everyone froze until Patch's howl ended and laughter erupted.

Jo gasped for air. "Patch's voice is even worse than Uncle Nick's."

Patch moved forward and nudged Nick's leg with his nose as if to apologize. Nick scratched him behind the ears. "Take a bow, Patch."

Patch lowered his front legs and dipped his head.

Kaitlyn pushed up from her chair. "I think it's time for bed."

A chorus of "no" and "not yet" rang out.

Clare must've also seen how exhausted Kaitlyn looked. "We'll send them up to bed in a bit."

Kaitlyn nodded and traipsed upstairs.

As she left, Ben asked, "How did you teach him to do that?"

Nick grabbed a handful of popcorn and helped Ben teach Patch a few basic tricks.

Elsie had distracted the other kids with some paper and pencils at the dining table, something about writing a Christmas pageant.

Once Ben heard that, he tugged Nick over to join in the fun at the table. Nick sidled up to Tillie, who was focusing hard on her paper, her tongue sticking out.

He couldn't help but observe her shaky letters. Her handwriting was really coming along. Except for one thing.

"Your lower case *d* should face the other direction. Like this." He drew it for her. Then he connected his left-hand fingers with his index finger up, making the shape of a *b*, then did the same in his right hand, except making a *d*. "Say the ABCs with me."

When she said *b* he held up his left-hand *b*, then when she said *d*, he held up his *d*.

He waved the *b* he made with his left hand. "Reading left to right, *b* comes first, so it faces this direction. '*D*' comes second, so it faces this direction."

"Oh!" Tillie scratched a new *d* on her page. Then another. And another.

Nick felt a tiny prick of pride that he'd helped. "Good work."

"How come you aren't a teacher like Miss Elsie, Uncle Nick?"

A hot ache expanded in his stomach at the innocent question.

Elsie looked up from across the table to watch him.

"I don't know." The words fell like stones from his mouth.

Isaac had asked him the very same thing. The answer had felt wrong when he'd said it to his brother, and it felt wrong now.

Tillie didn't seem to realize she'd stirred up a hornet's nest in his thoughts. "You're a good teacher, Uncle Nick," she said absently, already working again.

Five years ago, when he'd been expelled, he'd thought

his dream was over. Thought it was a sign his pa had been right, that schooling was a waste of time.

But what if he'd been wrong?

Thirteen

NICK WENT ON PATROL NOT LONG after Tillie's question had flipped him topsy-turvy. After trudging a wide circle through the snow-covered brush on the McGraw property for the last hour, Nick hadn't spotted anything out of the ordinary.

He couldn't tell whether the vague feeling of wrongness haunting him was because they still hadn't had word from his brothers or something else.

The snowscape expanded over the horizon, making him acutely aware of the miles between them and their closest neighbors. Patch walked by his side.

The barn loomed not far ahead. Bunkhouse a bit beyond that. Everything was still and quiet. Nick's head pounded.

He clenched and unclenched his hands, trying to bring some feeling back to his fingers.

Suddenly, Patch stopped short, hackles up, his nose pointed toward the southern horizon.

Nick looked to see what had alerted Patch. In the distance, a light flickered. Faint, but there. He blinked and it was gone.

He took his spyglass from his inside coat pocket and scanned the area until his eyes began to water.

He'd seen something. Where was it? What was it?

A rustling sounded in the snowy ground behind him. He lowered his spyglass and whipped around, reaching for the revolver at his hip.

Two silhouettes approached, too short to be a threat. "Uncle Nick," David whispered. Eli was right behind him.

Nick's heart thudded in his chest as he lowered his hand. What were his nephews doing out here?

He looked back to where he'd seen the light. It was still dark. Was someone out there?

Nick walked toward them. "What are you two doing? I thought you were in bed."

David dragged his toe through the snow. His words showed in the puff of moist air. "We couldn't sleep. We wanted to help you scout."

"You snuck out?"

David looked guilty, but Eli's chin jutted out. "We been cooped up in the house all day. We wanna help."

Kaitlyn and Clare would be furious to know the boys had snuck out.

An order for the boys to go back into the house was on the tip of Nick's tongue, but that light in the distance flickered once again. Only, this time on the north side of the house.

Unease skittered down his spine.

It couldn't be a coincidence, those two lights. Could it?

The McGraw property spread farther than the eye could see. If someone was out there, they were trespassing. And this time of night, whoever it was would be up to no good.

But Nick couldn't be in two places at once.

He tore his attention off the horizon and studied the boys. They were so young. "I need your help," he blurted.

This was dangerous. If something happened to one of these boys, he'd never forgive himself. Neither would his brothers.

Elsie believed in his ability to think things through. This was his only choice.

Nick clamped his hand on David's shoulder and turned the boy to where he'd seen the flicker. "See there?"

Eli hovered at their back, watching over David's shoulder. David nodded.

"That's over by the dried creek bed where you boys play hide-and-seek during the summer. I saw a light flash."

"I know lots of hiding spots over there, Uncle Nick," David said.

"I want you two to sneak over there and scout the area. Then come right back."

Eli was fairly bouncing on his toes. "Yes!"

Nick put out a hand to quiet the boy. "This isn't a game of hide-and-seek. There could be men out there who want to hurt you. Hear me? You are only to scout it out."

Both kids nodded. Nick hesitated for a moment, pulled his rifle out of the scabbard he'd slung across his back.

The warning his father had given him when he'd handed a rifle to Nick for the first time echoed through his head.

Nick held out his rifle to David. "Don't put your finger on the trigger unless you're willing to shoot."

David eyed the gun, quiet and serious now. His jaw twitched as he reached for it. "Just like you taught me, Uncle Nick."

"Meet back right here. Be careful."

They were gone, running through the snow and into the woods just moments later.

Nick's chest locked up.

Please, God, be with them.

Nick took a quick moment to settle Patch close to the house. The dog would bark an alert if anyone came close.

Then Nick hiked in the other direction.

The pulsing in his shoulder kept time with the pounding in his head. When was the last time he'd slept?

He pushed through the exhaustion, fighting through the snow drifts and trying to stay out of sight.

This was about protecting the people he loved.

Tillie's sweetly asked question popped into his mind again.

How come you aren't a teacher like Miss Elsie?

All the reasons he'd told himself years ago resonated like hollow excuses now.

Sure, he'd been framed, but he could've fought to have the truth revealed. Could've gone to a different school. Tried again.

Isaac had got him thinking about going back. Starting over.

He had never filed the paperwork to buy that land. What if he simply . . . didn't?

Drew had big plans to expand. Build the McGraw legacy. Someone would have to winter with the cattle. But what if Nick could still go back to school?

His head reeled over the revelation that he truly wanted to go back to school. Finish his teaching certification.

He couldn't deny it any longer. After this was all over, he would sit down with Drew. Talk things over. Make a plan. He might not know what to do about Elsie, but this path seemed clear.

Forcing his mind back to the present, he slowed as he climbed through the brush. A flash of light from ahead had him scurrying behind a tree for cover.

The form of a rider appeared in the distance, dark against the starry sky and snow-covered ground.

Two riders, carrying torches.

He pulled out his spyglass and looked through it.

Both men's faces were concealed with bandannas. By the way they carried themselves, they certainly weren't Nick's brothers.

An icy chill prickled under his skin. What were these men doing out here on McGraw land?

Nick sank into a kneel and watched, hoping to see some activity to prove the riders had a different purpose than what he feared.

The two men circled. Came close together, paced apart. What were they doing? Watching? For what?

Nick couldn't stay and watch all night. He needed to get back to the boys. Make sure they were all right.

He hated abandoning his post but had no choice.

With deliberate steps, he made his way back to the barn.

As he neared, Patch jumped up and came to his side with high-pitched whines.

"Hey, boy. Where are the kids?"

Patch circled Nick, agitated.

"David. Eli. Where are you?" he called quietly into the dark.

Dread snaked up his spine.

"David. Eli."

No answer.

His pulse galloped in his ears. Had they been caught by whoever was out there? Where were they?

His eyes scanned for any shadows moving.

Nothing. Wait—

Something crackled in the underbrush.

Nick whipped around. "David?"

He held his breath until he heard "It's us."

A relieved sigh whooshed out of Nick's lungs, and his eyes closed.

"Uncle Nick," Eli said. Nick peeled his eyes open to see the boys' drawn expressions. "We've got a problem."

Nick had been gone for too long.

Elsie stood at the counter, looking out the darkened window, even though it was impossible to see.

There was nothing left to clean in the kitchen, but Elsie kept up the pretense of scrubbing the spotless countertop anyway. Kaitlyn and the girls had gone up to bed. For a while, Rebekah and Clare had sat in the living room, making last-minute adjustments to Christmas gifts that had begun to appear beneath the decorated tree. Their voices had faded some time ago, and Elsie couldn't help but wonder whether she was the only one left awake in the entire house.

She missed Nick.

Somehow, over the last few days, she'd become keenly aware of his nearness. When he glanced up from across the room as she passed through, their eyes met. When she brushed past him as she served lunch at the table, she felt the shiver of awareness, knowing he was there, that he was watching her.

And now that he'd been gone so long this evening, his absence was like a pulsing heartbeat.

Where. Where. Where.

Where was he?

Faint light came from the front room. Elsie had left a lantern in the window, just in case. A beacon to cut through the dark night and guide Nick home. Should she light one here in the kitchen too? If only she knew which direction he would approach the house from.

Fabric rustled from the doorway, and she glanced over her shoulder to find Rebekah looking around the kitchen.

"I thought I left my mending basket in here." Her gaze landed on Elsie. She hesitated. "You all right?" Rebekah asked.

Elsie forced a smile. "I put it over here. I'm sorry, I should've brought it up to you."

She turned back, but Rebekah's attention had fixed on the window. Elsie saw the other woman's weariness in the drooping of her shoulders and her worry in the way she bit her lip.

Elsie handed her the basket. "Can I help with any mending?"

Rebekah's focus returned to Elsie. Her brows crinkled. "What are you—are you still cleaning up?"

"Not really . . ."

Rebekah accepted the basket as she glanced around the room. "You've cleaned up every little bit of the mess Tillie made helping with supper."

Elsie smoothed her empty hands down the pleat of her skirt. "It wasn't much—"

"And the paper scraps from Jo cutting snowflakes. And you've swept up David's pencil shavings." There was a note of exasperation in Rebekah's voice.

"I—" Elsie had done all of that. It hadn't been a hardship. She'd wanted something to keep her hands busy, even as her mind was busy worrying over Nick.

"You're a guest in our house, and this is how we're treating you?"

Elsie picked up the rag she'd abandoned on the counter and folded it. She didn't want to rile Rebekah any further.

"I didn't mind," Elsie admitted. "I actually—"

She clamped her mouth shut as a beat of awareness swept through her. How could she have forgotten who Rebekah was? These past hours as they'd wrangled the children together and shared concerns over what was happening with the other McGraw brothers, Elsie had begun to feel as if Rebekah was a friend.

But she wasn't.

Rebekah was a reporter. One who might spill Elsie's secrets to the entire town . . . and that could have disastrous consequences.

Rebekah must've seen her hesitation. Something shifted in her expression, a minute change that resulted in a fine tension in the air between them.

And Elsie felt a rush of uncertainty. Nick seemed to trust Rebekah. And Elsie dearly needed a friend.

She laid the rag on the sink. "Since you and Ed and Nick brought me here, I've felt like . . . felt like I've been home."

Rebekah's expression warmed.

It was more than that though, and suddenly Elsie felt herself swamped with emotion.

Bread. Bread would be nice at breakfast.

Elsie turned to the larder and pulled out a bag of flour. And words tumbled out before she could stop them. "My sister and I used to sing carols constantly during the days leading up to Christmas. Our father would grumble and protest, but if you watched him carefully, he'd smile when you weren't looking." She'd forgotten about that, right up until this moment.

Rebekah sidled next to her at the counter to help. "You have a beautiful singing voice."

"Oh, nothing like my sister's," Elsie protested quickly. "Darcy has the most beautiful voice. She could be a professional singer, on stage somewhere in the East. She's that good. Sometimes she'd ask me to sing in rounds with her, and we'd go faster and faster until I was so out of breath that I couldn't continue." And then both of them had collapsed in giggles.

"You love her very much," Rebekah said as she pulled down the mixing bowl from the shelf.

Elsie nodded.

"But you won't see her for Christmas?"

It should've been an easy question to answer. But Elsie hesitated again before divulging, "It's complicated. My mother is . . . my mother isn't easy. She and Darcy had a falling out a few years ago, and . . ."

Rebekah didn't look up as she added a portion of the starter into the mixing bowl. "And if you visit your sister at Christmas, your mother will make things difficult for you?"

Rebekah had cut to the heart of the matter even without all the details. Mother hadn't wanted Darcy to marry Reuben. Even before that, Darcy had chafed under Mother's "episodes" and the way she manipulated circumstances to suit her whims.

If Elsie visited Darcy and Reuben for the holiday, Mother would offer cutting words in her next letter to Elsie, would perhaps refuse to speak to her for a period of time.

And if Elsie went home to visit Mother and Father, she'd spend the whole time missing Darcy.

It was easier to stay away. At least she wouldn't make anyone unhappy.

Except herself, she was beginning to realize.

Elsie blinked away the heat building in her eyes and went to gather the oil from the larder.

Everything would change once Elsie wrangled the nerve to be able to tell Arnold she didn't want to see him romantically, didn't have any interest in marrying him. That was why she'd put it off for so long.

Mother and Father had chosen to take her in after her pa's abandonment, but if they decided to cut her out of their lives, who would she have left?

There was noise from the living room, and Elsie glimpsed a flash of Clare moving around.

Rebekah was opening her mouth to speak when something banged into the side of the house.

Elsie jumped. Rebekah did too, whirling so she had a view of the back door.

"What was that?" Rebekah whispered.

Something *scritch-scratched* on the porch. Was that—

It sounded like a dog's paws scrabbling for purchase.

"Patch?" Elsie whispered back to Rebekah.

But there was no sound of footsteps or Nick letting himself into the house.

"What if he pushed too hard and his head injury knocked him out?" Elsie's words to Rebekah were a frantic whisper.

Rebekah looked alarmed. "I thought he was better."

Elsie felt the same fear slither through her as she had when the doctor had explained the severity of Nick's injury. She knew he was still having headaches. He wasn't completely healed. What if . . .

Elsie edged toward the door. "If it's Patch—"

"What if it isn't?" Rebekah demanded.

Elsie reached for the nearest thing she could find—a sturdy rolling pin.

If Nick needed help, they couldn't just leave him—

She was reaching for the door's latch when there was a sudden rush of noise. Whispered voices from outside the door, rustling of clothes and footsteps.

"It's not Nick!" she whispered frantically to Rebekah, who waved her to retreat to the living room.

But it was too late—the door was already opening.

Elsie raised the rolling pin, fear nearly choking her.

And David and Eli tumbled inside.

Fourteen

SHOCK HELD ELSIE IMMOBILE FOR A moment as the two boys rushed inside, making about as much noise as two boys could. They stamped the snow from their feet and shucked their coats.

Nick was right behind them. Patch followed, then shook and skirted into the front room, probably to the warmth of his blankets.

Nick's eyes met hers as a wave of relief swamped her. He took her in at a glance, one eyebrow rising when he registered the rolling pin in her hand. She quickly thrust it onto the counter. He stood rigid, the tight set of his jaw betraying his upset.

Rebekah was moving toward the boys. "What in the world?" she asked at full volume.

Footsteps approached from the living room. Perhaps Clare was coming to reprimand everyone. It was as if they'd forgotten the rest of the household was asleep.

"We went to help Uncle Nick," Eli said with an almost belligerent tone and a jut of his chin.

"They snuck out," Nick said gravely.

Clare appeared in the doorway, mouth set. She must've heard what he'd said. "Eli Barlow!" There was no mistaking the fury in her voice, and Eli wilted a bit.

David ducked his head.

Was this the reason for the tension in Nick? Surely if he'd had to track down two energetic, ornery boys, he was half frozen and likely frightened for them.

Elsie moved toward the stove. Coffee. A pot of hot coffee would warm Nick up and maybe erase the tightness around his mouth.

"We helped!" Eli protested, though it was a little weaker than his first statement.

Water. Coffee beans.

Elsie listened even as she checked items off on the list in her mind. She bent to check the fire in the stove, stirred it a little.

"Can you douse the lamp in the other room?" Nick asked Rebekah, and the sense of urgency in his voice sent the other woman scurrying to do what he'd asked.

"What's wrong?" Elsie asked Nick.

His eyes flicked in her direction, but then he spoke to Clare. "They did help," he said grimly. "There were men on our property—more than one and in more directions than I could scout."

Eli's chest puffed out now. "We sneaked up on 'em and watched a couple of riders out past the gully."

Clare stood with one hand pressed against her mouth.

Elsie couldn't tell from the way her eyes had narrowed whether she was frightened or angry. Perhaps both.

David piped in. "Then another guy came, and we followed him for a while too."

Rebekah rushed back into the room.

Elsie's heart was pounding in her throat, the coffee momentarily forgotten. There were men on the McGraw property? At night?

"Go upstairs and wake your sisters," Nick told David. "Tell them to get their shoes on."

"Want me to get Ben?" Eli could hardly contain his excitement, oblivious to the tension between the adults in the room.

"Fine," Clare murmured with a wave of her hand. The boys raced out of the room. Clare followed at a walk.

Rebekah looked to Nick. "It wasn't your brothers?"

He shook his head tightly. "Can Kaitlyn ride?" he asked her.

Rebekah shook her head. "She's been nauseated all day. Can't keep much down. She's weak and she'd probably get dizzy in the saddle."

And a fall from the back of a horse could injure both her and the baby.

"A wagon is too slow," he murmured to himself.

The coffeepot began to boil with a slight rattle, and Elsie turned by rote to take it off the stove and pour water into the cups she'd already set out.

Her mind was racing. If Nick wanted Kaitlyn to ride, that meant he thought they should run away. Terror made her hands shake as she imagined riding through the night in complete darkness.

Clare returned to the room and laid two rifles on the worktable. As Elsie watched, she pulled several bullets from her apron pocket and dropped them on the table with a tinkling rattle.

"How many men?" Clare asked as she used a lever to open the chamber of one of the rifles and began feeding a bullet inside.

"At least eight, if the boys counted right."

Clare's lips were pressed into a tight line. "I'm not finished being angry with you for putting them in harm's way."

He didn't look away from the fury in her low voice. "I wish I hadn't had to."

Elsie felt the beat of shame that matched the tone of his voice. Nick couldn't move fast enough, not with his injuries. He couldn't be in two places at once.

"We can't stay here," he said.

"Kaitlyn can't go," Clare said. "You want to leave her behind?"

"No!"

Everything was moving too fast. Elsie sagged against the counter, fear making her quail.

"It's you and Elsie they want, isn't it?" Clare asked in a matter-of-fact manner. "Why don't the two of you make a run for it?"

"No," Nick repeated, this time with a stiff jaw.

"You can get help—"

"I said no!" This answer was thunderous, and Elsie felt as shocked as Clare looked.

Elsie had never heard Nick raise his voice before.

His eyes flicked to Elsie for only a brief second, and she felt the connection between them in that heartbeat.

Rapid footsteps sounded overhead. The girls were up.

Rebekah called downstairs, and Clare gave Nick a worried look before she left the room.

Elsie grabbed one of the cups of coffee and moved to Nick's side, offering it to him.

"Slow down and think," she said quietly. "You're one of the most intelligent men I know. You can figure this out."

His jaw tensed. "If I take time to think, then we'll all be dead."

She pushed the cup into his hand, though she didn't know whether he really registered that he'd taken it. "I don't understand."

He made a move toward the window, peering outside. He sipped the coffee, speaking quickly. "When I was about Eli's age, Pa took all four of us boys on a cattle drive, and I was sent ahead to drive the herd." He shook his head, clearly disappointed in himself for choices from the past. "I slowed down, trying to decide between two routes. Fell too far back. Took too much time thinking on which trail might be faster. I lost control of the herd and couldn't turn the cattle away from a rocky slope."

His eyes slid closed. "Because I wasn't where I needed to be, because I hesitated, some of the stock got injured. One so badly it had to be put down. It was a lean year, and we couldn't afford to lose any head. Pa said I was the weak link."

Oh, Nick.

Elsie's heart hurt for the boy he'd been. For the pain his father's words must've caused—still did. A young boy shouldn't have to bear such a heavy burden.

He looked at her, and she saw the fire inside him, this shame from the past burning him up even now. "I can't let my family, the people I care about, be injured or—killed"—he barely breathed the word—"because I'm thinking too slowly."

"Everyone makes mistakes," she whispered. "Imagine if it was Eli. Or David. Would you be angry with them?"

She saw the way his jaw worked as he cut his gaze away so his focus was on the window again. "Maybe."

She'd already seen the way he'd blamed himself for sending the boys to do a man's job. Thank God David and Eli were safe.

"You have to forgive yourself," she said. "I'm sure your father did, even if he didn't say so."

He stared at her and blinked, as if forgiving himself was a foreign concept.

"This family needs you to take a breath and think. Don't you see? That's your role. How you fit."

She saw the tiny shake of his head in his reflection in the darkened window. Had he held on to this pain for all these years?

He rubbed a hand down his face. "No amount of thinking is going to change this. We need help."

His brows creased after he said the words, his eyes narrowing in a way that meant his mind was working.

Since they'd been thrown back together, she'd witnessed

the real Nick McGraw. The protective, fun uncle. The loyal brother. The intelligent teacher.

She was falling in love with him all over again.

A voice rang out from upstairs. "Uncle Nick! They're coming!"

She jumped.

He turned from the window. Put the coffee cup on the counter. "We need help. That's the answer."

Clare ran back into the room, already reaching for one of the rifles.

He motioned to the window. "The neighbors'll come if there's a fire. A big inferno they can see for miles."

Elsie's heart thundered in her chest. "You're going to burn down the house?"

Nick shook his head, mind still working. "We need the hay in the barn to make it through the winter—Drew will want to keep the house."

Clare looked between them, eyes wide.

Nick's eyes caught Elsie's and held. "But the bunkhouse could go," he said.

Elsie saw his determination. If someone was even now riding toward the house, guns drawn, how could he think about going out into the night? She whirled and pressed her hands onto the counter. She could see the bunkhouse from the kitchen window. But it was so far away . . .

Clare and Nick were speaking in low murmurs, plans for something at the front door, but Elsie's mind had tuned out the sound.

She hadn't told him that her feelings for him had changed. How could she let him walk out of the house—

By the time she turned around, Nick was already moving toward the back door and the lean-to beyond.

"Wait!" She crossed the room after him, reached for him when he turned to her. Faltered when she fell into the intensity of his eyes. "Nick, I—"

He lowered his head and kissed her.

She stretched up on tiptoe to meet his kiss, let her hands slide behind his neck as waves of emotion broke over her.

Nick wasn't kissing her because he'd forgotten their past, because he was muddled by amnesia.

This kiss was real.

And over too soon.

She was aware of Clare still in the room as Nick pulled away, and the reality of what she'd done crashed over her. Her cheeks burned.

Nick gave her one more intense look before he rushed through the door into the lean-to. Running into danger.

All she could do was breathe a prayer he'd return.

Nick forced his whirling mind off Elsie's kiss and into focus as he pulled on his coat in the coolness of the lean-to.

He knew their neighbors. The Landerses and the Wilsons. Even though it was the middle of the night, they would come.

But would they get here in time?

Nick's shoulder flared with pain as he reached up to the shelf where they kept an extra lantern. His fingers fumbled with the box of matches. Tucking the matches into his pocket, he moved over to the corner and grabbed the can of kerosene.

Please, God, let this work.

He hesitated only a moment with one hand on the door's latch. Had he given Clare enough time to get ready?

He knew she wouldn't let him down. Could imagine her and Eli ducked low, waving the broomstick and dress out the front door, on the opposite side of the house.

The distraction would likely only buy him a few seconds.

He had to make it count.

He whistled as loud as he could, hoped the sound carried through the wall. And pushed the door open, darted through it, his feet crunching through the snow as his legs pumped.

Gunshots rang out from the woods in front of the house.

An answering shot came from an upstairs window. David?

The wound in his shoulder pulsed. He strained to hear over the heartbeats in his ears.

Another shot rang out from around the side of the house. This one zinged just overhead and slapped into the wall of the bunkhouse as Nick approached at a full run.

Only a few more feet . . .

A man's shout.

Nick couldn't take the time to look over his shoulder, see where the danger was coming from.

Another bullet whizzed past his ear. Too close.

With his last bit of energy, he forced a final burst of speed into his legs, ducking behind the corner of the bunkhouse as bullets slapped into the building. It was dark here. He'd be harder to see.

He put his back to the wall, hot pain swelling through his shoulder. Letting the can drop to the ground, he gripped his arm. His head whirled as he fought to catch his breath. Elsie had told him what the doc had said about pushing too hard. Pain pierced behind his right eye.

He closed his eyes, trying to steady himself. Memories of Elsie pressed in. The way she'd believed in him when she'd said *Your family needs you. That's your role.* The emotion in her eyes just before she'd kissed him.

The night had gone quiet, the men no longer firing. His harsh breaths were the only sound.

Were the men moving on the house? Surely Clare and David would be firing on them if that was the case.

He couldn't stop moving. He had to finish this.

Determination pushing him, he bent low and crawled to the opposite corner of the building.

This side of the bunkhouse had been dried out by the sun. The snow had even melted in blotches around the foundation. It was the best chance to start the fire.

The pungent oil of the kerosene assaulted his nostrils as he drenched the dried timbers at the base of the bunk-house.

He pulled out a match, his fingers trembling. Once lit, he wouldn't have a lot of time to get away from the inferno.

A man's voice shouted from somewhere nearby. Nick was out of time.

He struck the match and flicked it into the puddle of

kerosene. The tiny flame burst into a much larger one, illuminating the darkness with an orange glow.

Illuminating Nick.

A bullet thunked into the ground not far from Nick's boot. A second one slapped into the wall just past his side.

With fire crackling between him and the building, he made to run for the woods—but a spray of bullets blocked his path.

He zigzagged and ran around the side of the bunkhouse, conscious of the fact that there could be another man waiting there to take him out.

Behind him, the fire crackled hotter. He could feel the heat radiating off it now.

Before he reached the corner, more shots echoed from in front of him.

He was surrounded.

The bunkhouse door was just in front of him—his only escape.

He knocked into it with the full force of his body, almost falling inside as a bullet blasted into the wood just above his head. He kicked the door shut behind him.

Inside, he scanned the room for any way to escape. Smoke swirled in the long room lined with bunks. The blaze lighting up the sky outside hadn't caught inside yet.

The glass from the window opposite him shattered and he ducked. Bullet? Or had heat from the fire caused it to break?

It was warm inside. Too warm. He started sweating underneath his coat. Rubbed the back of one hand across his forehead, almost knocking his hat off.

He coughed once, squinting against the flickering, shadowy light coming in through the window. The smoky air burned his throat.

If he'd hoped for some magic answer to appear, he was sorely disappointed. How could he get away from the bunkhouse when it was surrounded, when the men outside wanted him dead and wouldn't hesitate to shoot?

He briefly considered whether he could lift one of the straw tick mattresses, use it as a shield—

Another bullet cracked through the wall, leaving a round hole behind, though luckily it was wide of Nick.

If the bullets were tearing through wood, the straw tick wouldn't offer enough protection. Nor was he certain he could lift and hold it—not with his bum shoulder.

A flame burst through one corner where the ceiling met the wall, quickly spreading across the ceiling like water running down a hill. The roof must be ablaze outside. Smoke had spread across the entire room and was dropping fast, blocking Nick's sight and causing another coughing fit, this one so bad that he had to bend over and grip his knees for support as his body shook.

If only he'd made it to the woods.

Now he was trapped. No way out.

Elsie's words from earlier hit him. *Take a breath and think.*

When he tried to breathe, it turned into a cough. The way his body convulsed made new pain radiate through his shoulder.

He crossed the room to the window, staying as low as he could. From a spot beside the window, he tried to peer through the flames and darkness. Drew his revolver and aimed it out the window, just in case.

Heat from the wall seared his skin, driving him a few steps back from the window.

He heard her voice in his head. *You're one of the most intelligent men I know. You can figure this out.*

Tears dripped down his cheeks as he fought against the smoke. Raising his forearm to shield his face from the smoke didn't help.

Come on, Nick. Think.

Flames climbed the wall to his left.

At least one good thing had come of this. He'd created an inferno that would be visible for miles.

Please, God, let help come. Fast.

He had to go back outside. Maybe the shooters would miss. At least if he ran to the woods, he'd have a chance. Staying inside meant burning alive.

The haze of smoke was so low now that he holstered his gun and crawled on his hands and knees.

A loud splintering sounded overhead, and he had only a split second to react. He rolled away just as part of the roof collapsed—blocking the door.

He wasn't going to make it.

He pressed his face into the floor, seeking one clean breath so he could *think*. Another coughing fit grabbed hold of him, and black spots danced before his eyes.

He didn't want to die like this.

He loved Elsie. Had never stopped loving her. Even when he hadn't been able to remember the previous day, his heart had remembered her.

The thought landed in his mind with perfect clarity, causing a ripple like a pebble dropped in a still lake.

He loved her.

And he wasn't going to get to tell her.

No.

He refused to have things end like this.

He rolled onto his back as he hacked and wheezed, looking for any other way—

The window.

The window on the north side of the building was untouched. Nick scrambled to his knees, lunged across the room. He hooked his hand onto the windowsill and wrenched his body up.

Flames licked the wall, moving closer.

He shoved open the window, heat from the glass scorching his bare palms.

With one great heave, he threw his body out the window, rolled away from the building, from the fire. Snow tingled against his face and hands even as he braced for a bullet, tried to find strength in his shaky legs to stand up. To run.

But the bullet never came.

Several shots rang out near the house.

No!

He pushed to his forearms, but another coughing fit kept him from getting up.

The house. He had to get to the house.

Just as he caught his breath and tried to catch a glimpse of the house past the burning bunkhouse, a horse thundered up only feet away, blocking his view.

"Little brother, who said you could have all the fun?"

Isaac.

"You're late," Nick croaked before he let himself go limp, face down in the snow.

Fifteen

NICK'S LIMBS TREMBLED AS ISAAC helped him to his feet.

"You shot?" Isaac asked.

Nick couldn't force his scorched throat to respond, so he shook his head. He let Isaac drag him to the cover of the barn as two riders raced through the yard on horseback.

The heat of the inferno radiated around him, but the farther Isaac helped him move away, the cooler the air lapping at his skin.

In the distance, a man on horseback chased another man, but another coughing fit blurred his sight.

Where was Elsie? Where was the family?

He dug his heels into the ground. "What about Elsie? The kids?"

Those few words made him double over, coughing. His shoulder pulled. Isaac hauled him up, kept them both moving.

"Drew and Ed went to the house to check on everyone. Marshal heard about the dustup in town and rode out to check on us—met us at the edge of Quade's property."

"Marshal O'Grady is here?"

"Just got back. And none too soon."

Some of the tension in Nick's neck eased. But until he saw Elsie for himself, felt her in his arms, he wouldn't relax.

Isaac steered him toward the barn, but Nick's eyes remained on the house. "The house—"

"Nobody made it to the house. Clare was firing shots to keep them back when we rode up." Pride in Isaac's voice. "Half of them had you covered at the bunkhouse."

Isaac leaned Nick against the barn wall, and Nick couldn't stop from sinking to the cool ground.

Nick could still hear the ruckus of men fighting over the blaze of flames. The pounding of hoofbeats as the bad guys were rounded up.

The soot lining Nick's lungs burned. His chest convulsed with a cough he tried to contain, but it burst out. And it wouldn't stop.

"I'll get you some water as soon as I can," Isaac said, kneeling over him, his brow knit tight.

Nick sipped in air as the cough subsided. Pain coursed down every nerve in his arm.

Isaac examined him, looking for bullet wounds. "You've got a bad habit of getting shot at, little brother. We saw the smoke as we were heading to check out an old dugout west of Eagle Creek. You did good."

Nick's breath hitched. It had worked. Nick had kept the family safe.

But his smoke signal had come at a high cost of McGraw property. The bunkhouse was a total loss.

Isaac examined the old wound on Nick's head.

Shouts echoed in the night, the words disappearing into the roar of the diminishing flames.

Not far from the house, Nick could make out a group of men being surround by his brothers and other townsmen Nick couldn't recognize in the dim light. One smaller form—Marshal O'Grady?—gave instructions to someone with a rope. The man roughly tied the criminal's hands behind his back as other lawmen followed suit.

Horses scattered across the field, but the threat appeared to be under control.

Over by the bunkhouse, shadows of people formed a bucket brigade, dousing the angry flames before the sparks reached any other building. He thought he recognized David in the distance, and the kid next to David might be Eli.

Nick searched for Elsie but couldn't see her in the flickering light. He hoisted himself up, but his head rushed, and he caught himself against the barn wall.

Isaac sidled next to him and supported him with an arm around his torso. "Let's get you inside."

Nick nodded. If that was where Elsie was, then he wanted to be there too.

Together, Isaac and Nick made their way to the house, passing the group of men whose tin stars glinted in the firelight as they surrounded the scowling bandits.

Isaac slowed, taking a closer look at the men in the center. Nick wanted to count them, but his head hurt too much.

Isaac's mouth tightened into a grim line. "Quade's not here."

Nick heard what Isaac wasn't saying. If Quade wasn't among those captured, he was still out there.

Nick's gaze snagged on the silhouette of a man pouring another bucket onto the flames lapping up the bunkhouse. Drew.

He wanted to go over, apologize, tell Drew he hadn't known how else to call for help. But his feet stuck to the ground.

The destruction of the bunkhouse felt like another example of how he was still the weak link.

A lump formed in his throat.

He should at least go help with the brigade.

He started that way, but a hand clamped onto his shoulder, stopping him.

Ed. "It's almost out. They can handle it."

Nick's chest squeezed as he took in the simmering posts and planks, now black. "I wish I'd had another choice."

Ed didn't say anything for a minute, watching the form of Rebekah step down from the porch and come toward him. "Nick, I'd rather have my wife than that old bunkhouse. You saved them all."

A sting nipped at the back of Nick's eyes.

Ed clapped Nick on the back, then crossed the remaining distance to meet Rebekah with a long kiss. Then they turned and watched the bunkhouse, now a heap of ash and debris, smolder.

Next to Nick, Isaac also watched, his arms crossed over

his chest. Drew paced the length of the disintegrated wall, a bucket in his hand, looking for hot spots.

Memories stirred of Nick bunking in there with his brothers. Together. Before wives. Before grown-up responsibilities. Memories that weighed heavy.

How many conversations rang within those walls? The roughhousing his mom would never allow inside their home. The bunkhouse represented their family legacy. Their past.

It would never be like that again.

With a sigh, he turned back toward the house. Next to him, Isaac helped him keep his balance.

As they neared the porch, Clare ran outside and threw herself at Isaac. "I thought something had happened to you." Her voice shook.

Nick held on to the railing for support. Where was Elsie?

She appeared in the open doorway, a gust flaring her skirt. She stared at him with a haunted look in her eyes. Until her face crumpled.

He used the railing to haul himself up the porch steps. She met him at the top.

When he opened his arm, she tucked herself into his chest.

He pressed his face into her hair. He couldn't even care that he was getting her all sooty. She was all right.

She sucked in a trembling breath and eased out of his arms.

"Are you hurt? Did I hurt your shoulder? Your head? I just—"

Her eyes shone with unshed tears, studying him.

She went still, and he reached up to smooth her hair behind her ears. "Nothing hurts right now. Not while you're looking at me like that."

Pink flushed her cheeks. She was looking at him with such vulnerability. Everything had changed over the past few days.

"Come inside. You're cold, and you'll catch your death."

"You're so bossy."

Yet neither one of them moved. If the night had taught him anything, it was that tomorrow was never guaranteed.

"I need to talk to you—"

"There's something I need to say—"

He cut off when she spoke at the same time. She ducked her head shyly and he chuckled.

He squeezed her hand. "You go first."

A long moment passed as she seemed to gather herself. She looked up into his face. "Can we start over?"

Elsie watched emotions flicker across Nick's face, afraid to move or even breathe. There was chaos all around.

She was aware of Isaac and Clare at the foot of the stairs, deputies loading up the bandits on horses nearby. A few men still stood around the debris, throwing buckets on hotspots. Yet it felt like she and Nick were in their own little world.

Nick was opening his mouth to respond when another voice intruded.

"Miss Atchison, what are you doing here?"

Elsie knew that voice. She became instantly aware of

Nick's hands at her waist, how close they stood. She stepped away and twisted to face the ruddy-faced man she hadn't heard approach. What was a member of the school board doing way out here?

Her throat swelled until she could hardly force out words. "Mr. Jamison. What are you doing here?"

He stared at her suspiciously. "I volunteered as deputy. You didn't answer my question."

The man's eyes snagged on Elsie's hands, where Nick's hand had closed around hers. Disapproval flashed in his eyes.

Nick stepped close to her side. "Ed and I brought her here for protection after she witnessed an attempted murder. The marshal was gone from town."

The suspicion hadn't faded. "Did you tell any of the board members your whereabouts? It is our duty to help protect your reputation." His gaze zeroed in on their clasped hands. "Or perhaps your intention isn't to teach next year."

It was clear from his words he meant something else entirely.

"School's on break," Nick said tightly. "Elsie can go where she likes."

The man's mouth tightened into a grim line. "Certainly, but as you know, it is important that our teacher's reputation is above reproach. Rumors could spread with her so far from town."

Nick lifted his chin in a challenge. "Are you implying something, Mr. Jamison?"

Elsie felt a tremor go through Nick, lines of exhaustion

around his eyes and mouth. He hadn't slept all night. He needed rest, but he wasn't backing down.

"You two go inside." Marshal Danna O'Grady shooed them as she climbed the porch steps.

Relief splashed over Elsie, but it was short-lived as Nick ushered her inside, Danna following.

Elsie's cheeks felt hot compared to the cold outside. Nick still shivered.

On shaky legs, Elsie hurried to the quilt rack in the corner of the room. "I'll get a quilt."

She passed Ed and Rebekah talking to Drew in low tones. Kaitlyn bustled in the kitchen, Tillie not leaving her side as the scent of coffee wafted through the kitchen door.

Elsie was thankful for a moment to gather her strength with her back turned to the bustling room.

Jamison being here was a disaster. She had hugged Nick—not in a platonic way. Jamison's words about not teaching next year had been a clear allusion to her marrying Nick—and losing her position because of it.

Merritt had given up the job, had known Calvin wouldn't want a married teacher. But Elsie wanted to teach. That's why she'd put off Arnold's suit.

Arnold!

She'd never answered his letter. She'd been isolated out here, imagining herself a part of the McGraw Christmas traditions. Being protected by Nick.

But now her life was intruding.

What was she going to do?

"Have a seat, Nick, before you fall down," Ed demanded.

Elsie forced herself to turn back around. The lantern

light illuminated Nick's tight features. Pain reflected in his eyes. Soot layered every inch of his skin. A gash in his cheek trickled blood through the soot and down his neck.

Oh, Nick.

Elsie's mind still whirled as she returned to Nick and tucked the quilt around him.

In the corner, Marshal O'Grady joined Ed and motioned for Drew to join them. Rebekah was ushering the kids upstairs. Not one of them argued.

Elsie turned to follow them upstairs, but Nick reached out and grabbed her hand. "Stay."

She should refuse. This seemed like a brothers' meeting, but Nick's eyes pleaded with her. Almost like he needed her. She lowered onto the settee next to him before she could think better of it. He didn't let go of her hand.

The kitchen door opened, and Isaac walked through carrying two cups of coffee. He handed one to Nick, who accepted the mug, then settled back into the couch, exhaustion lining his face.

Marshal O'Grady's expression was grim. "The hired guns jumped at the chance to reduce their sentence by implicating Quade."

Relief flooded Elsie. It would mean another charge against him, wouldn't it?

"We just need to find him," Danna said.

Elsie tensed and Nick squeezed her hand. "He wasn't with the hired guns," he whispered.

Elsie glanced at Ed, who lifted his mug toward his mouth. The worry lines on his face told her it was true.

The more desperate Quade became, the more unpredictable he would be.

"We've got all these men deputized, so let's go find him," Isaac suggested.

Danna nodded. "I'll have to send a few to take the hired guns to Calvin but can spare half to go after Quade."

The men nodded and started breaking away.

Tillie ran back downstairs, as if she'd been listening. "I don't want you to leave, Papa."

Drew scooped her up, speaking quietly.

Nick didn't move. "You don't want to go?" Elsie whispered.

His eyes were intense. "I've got a good reason to stay."

Elsie's heart leaped. They hadn't finished their conversation.

Before Elsie could move, Marshal O'Grady pulled away from the group and approached Elsie. "Jamison seems to be on a warpath. Wants you back in town."

It came as no surprise, but Elsie still couldn't stop her pulse from quickening.

Nick leaned forward. "Elsie's on Christmas break."

The marshal's eyes flickered. "I've been in your shoes," she said to Elsie. "City council watching my every move. I learned sometimes it's not about what I had a right to do but what would keep the peace."

Nick's frown deepened.

All the thoughts that had spun up when Elsie had come inside still churned. The only thing she could really lean on was her job.

She smoothed her hands down her skirt and stood. "She's right. I should go."

Nick pushed to his feet. "Then I'm coming too. Quade's still out there."

"No," she said quickly. A flash of hurt crossed his face.

"Can you give us a minute?" he asked. Danna gave a nod, then stepped outside.

Nick rubbed the back of his neck. "I don't like this."

"I need my job," she blurted.

Everything had happened so quickly in the past few days. Tensions had been high. Nick had loved her again—while his memories had been gone. She needed time.

A minute shadow crossed behind his eyes. "I understand." Determination flattened his lips. "But you asked me a question earlier. I'd wanted to ask you the same question."

Her heart fluttered. Had she heard right? "You want to start over? You forgive me?"

"We both made mistakes. Can you forgive me for walking away?"

Elsie inhaled to keep from crying, but one tear escaped, trailing down her cheek.

With featherlike gentleness, he wiped it away. "So, what do you say? Can we start over?"

She wanted to lean into his touch. But footsteps thudded on the floor above them. They weren't alone. Maybe it was a good thing. "I think we already have. But Nick, I have to go back to town. I need some time."

The shadows in his expression had cleared. "I've got some things to work out too, but I'd like to come courting, if you're willing. Do things the right way this time. Out in the open."

Elsie smiled. "No more sneaking around?"

"No more sneaking around," he whispered back.

"And no more stolen kisses?" she whispered again.

This time, a rakish glint shone in his eyes. "Well, maybe one more." The words were barely spoken he was so close.

His lips brushed hers. This kiss was real. Nick and Elsie.

Distantly, she registered the back door opening and muffled voices in the kitchen.

Elsie should step back but couldn't take her eyes off Nick. He watched her with that crooked grin she'd always loved.

"I don't know how long it's gonna take, but I'll come to you as soon as I can." There was a promise in Nick's words.

"I'll be waiting."

Sixteen

ELSIE STOOD BEHIND HER TEACHER desk piled with pine branches, absently tying the boughs together to drape around her classroom.

It was Christmas Eve. The school term might be over, but she and Merritt had only had a few hours to prepare for the town's Christmas social, which the schoolhouse hosted every year. The midday sun shone into the room, warming away the winter chill.

And she couldn't focus. Not since Rebekah had visited earlier with news that Nick should be arriving sometime that evening.

Quade was still at large, and Elsie was aware of the deputy standing on guard outside, his tall silhouette just outside the window.

"Is this wreath centered?"

Elsie glanced up at Merritt, who stood on a ladder, holding a wreath above the chalkboard.

"Close enough," Elsie answered.

Merritt must've agreed, because she started to tap a nail into the wall.

Elsie couldn't wait to see Nick. Hearing he could arrive that evening made her heart soar. And pinched her stomach into a tight coil.

It had been four long, grueling days since she'd last seen Nick.

What had he been doing? What was he thinking?

She missed him.

And she still questioned how things would work between them. They'd agreed to start over, but he'd made no promises.

And she hadn't forgotten he'd asked Merritt to find him a wife.

The ladder rattled as Merritt stepped down. "There'll be a school board meeting in the first part of January."

Elsie swallowed a groan. Why had Merritt brought that up? It only made Elsie recall the lecture on propriety she'd received from Mr. Jamison the whole way to town the night of the fire.

Merritt unrolled a spool of ribbon. "Should I suggest to the school board to start looking for a new schoolmarm for next year?"

Elsie stilled. "What? Why?"

Merritt raised an eyebrow as she formed the ribbon into a bow.

Oh. She was talking about Nick.

Elsie picked up the bough and resumed her work. "Merritt, I love teaching. I love how the kids' eyes light up when they finally understand, or how they take a hold of a concept and make it their own. Their sweet little gifts of wildflowers, and . . . and . . ."

"Being married is wonderful too." Merritt's voice had softened but was unapologetic.

Why couldn't Elsie do both? Why couldn't she keep teaching and marry Nick at the same time?

Merritt tied her bow onto the pine garland. "Have you finished your letter to Mr. Nelson?"

Elsie shook her head. After Merritt had taken her in, Elsie had told her dear friend everything. Falling for Nick five years ago, the breakup, life, her parents pushing her toward Arnold.

Merritt spoke kindly. "Elsie. Problems don't simply disappear."

"I know. But Mother will be so angry." And she owed the Westons so much.

A knock on the door interrupted further conversation.

Elsie looked at the clock, heart leaping. It was still early afternoon. Was Nick here already?

She couldn't contain the bubble of excitement rising inside of her as she smoothed her hair into place and moved toward the door.

She swung the door open wide.

But it wasn't Nick on the other side.

As if their conversation had conjured him, Arnold Nelson stood before her wearing an expectant smile, looking dapper with his hat in his hand. The sight of him doused Elsie's heart with icy water.

Her smile faded. "Arnold?"

It was jarring to see him here. Out of place in the doorway of her schoolroom.

Arnold's smile didn't falter. He stepped over the threshold, one hand reaching for her. "Darling."

"Wh-what are you doing here?" she stammered, backing up a step.

He dropped his hand when he realized she hadn't taken it. His attention flickered across the room. "It's just how you described it in your letters. It has been too long. I've missed you." He stepped toward her, reaching out again.

Panic swelled and she took another step away.

I want to start over. Nick's words played in her mind.

In this moment, with her feelings for Nick at the forefront of her thoughts, it couldn't be more obvious to Elsie that she and Arnold would never work.

What she felt for him was platonic friendship. Nothing more. What should she do now?

Awkwardness rose between them as he stared expectantly.

Merritt cleared her throat, and Arnold turned toward her as she fiddled with a bow in her hand.

He smiled. "I was so entranced with Elsie that I hadn't realized someone else was in the room. Hello, I'm Arnold."

Merritt nodded, but her eyes directed a message toward Elsie. "Elsie's mentioned you."

His smile broadened. "Did she?"

Arnold's focus came right back to Elsie. "I read in the paper about the terrible blizzard, and I simply couldn't wait until the New Year to see you. I was worried you'd be stranded or need help."

Elsie's stomach knotted. "We should talk." Courage built in her chest.

But before she could speak, he held out a letter. "From your parents. We had an early Christmas dinner before I left. They send their love." He had attended Christmas dinner with her folks? Perhaps it was Mother who'd insisted Arnold come to see her. Was this entire meeting part of Mother's machinations?

Last time Mother had written, she'd touted Arnold's good qualities, hinted that he would make a good husband for Elsie.

And Arnold's last letter had laid out his feelings on paper.

This was all Elsie's fault. She'd waited too long to say something.

She raised a trembling hand and accepted the letter.

Words stuck in her throat, the weight of her parents' expectations suffocating.

"You look a little peaked, darling. Have you eaten?" He glanced toward Merritt. "Do you mind if I steal her away? Let's go for a late lunch. I need to speak with you privately."

Elsie met Merritt's stare until she felt Arnold settle her coat over her shoulders. Then he escorted her out the door before she could protest.

She tried to rally herself.

Bossy.

Nick's voice in her head again. Why was it so hard with Arnold?

Outside, the sun shone brightly, melting snow into a slushy, muddy mess. Mrs. Steele from the café peeked through the curtains. Did a double take.

Elsie walked beside Arnold along the boardwalk, though she didn't take his arm. The woman probably wondered who the man with the new schoolteacher was.

A family bustled down the boardwalk across the street, their eyes following her. She folded her arms around her stomach.

He glanced down at her arms. "I know it's been too long since we've been together, but you don't have to feel shy around me, Elsie. You can't imagine how happy I am to see you."

"I'm always happy to see a friend."

He studied her. "I do believe that after all this time, you are lovelier than ever."

She couldn't meet his gaze. He sounded so sincere. But she felt nothing from his words.

She swallowed hard. "You should've seen me before the Christmas pageant. My frazzled state looked more like I was caught in an electrical storm. Hair sticking up everywhere."

He laughed. "Oh, Elsie, you can make me laugh."

Her breath lodged in her chest as he swung in front of her, halting her mid-stride. Before she could stop him, he grasped both her hands in his, not caring who saw.

"It's time that we make this official, Elsie." His voice carried.

A swell of panic clenched her gut. She tried to yank her hands free, but his grip tightened. His expression was intent.

"Arnold, stop."

In the distance, almost buried by the rushing in her ears,

she heard the gasps of nearby observers and the clop of hooves as someone rode up on the street, reining nearby.

Arnold didn't hear her protest as he released one hand to pull a small box from his coat pocket and open it to a silver ring. A wedding ring? "The moment I saw you again, I knew. I can't wait any longer."

No, she couldn't let him do this. Elsie tried again to pull away the hand he still held, but he wouldn't budge. She couldn't bear to look and see who was watching.

"A match between us would make both our parents so happy. And it would certainly make me the happiest man on earth. Please, be my bride."

"Elsie?"

Everything went still. Only one voice could cut through the panic sweeping through her.

Nick had come.

And seen everything.

Nick stood frozen at the edge of the boardwalk. For a moment, he couldn't make sense of what he was seeing. And hearing.

Be my bride.

He felt as if he'd been shot all over again, pain bursting in his chest.

Another man gripped the hands of the woman Nick loved, holding a velvet box with a silver ring shining in the sun. Proposing to her.

For a beat, Nick waited. Waited for Elsie to demand he

explain himself. Reject his proposal. Did she even know this dandy?

But she seemed frozen in place, looking up into the face of the tall city slicker.

"Elsie, who is this?" The words tumbled from Nick's mouth, his thoughts scrambling to make sense of what he was seeing.

Elsie turned, eyes flaring wide and panicked. "Nick!"

"What is going on?" he demanded. The familiar burn of betrayal raged inside him. "Who is this?"

The stranger turned, still clasping that ring box. He eyed Nick, as if weighing whether he was a friend or a foe. "Arnold Nelson. Elsie's intended."

Again, Nick waited for her to refute him. Instead, he saw her mouth open and close like she couldn't find words. Saw the guilt and misery in her expression.

Nelson was telling the truth.

The man's fancy suit, the expensive coat, the beaver-skin hat—they all shouted *money*, made the fabric of Nick's Sunday best chafe against his skin.

Nelson wasn't from around here, and he came from money. More money than Nick would see in a lifetime.

I want to start over.

The words that Elsie had said ran through Nick's whirling thoughts. If that was true, then who was this?

Nick knew she'd had a life after they'd parted ways. But in the days they'd spent trapped together on the McGraw ranch, she'd never mentioned a beau.

Elsie took a faltering step toward him. "I-I can explain. I was expecting you later."

She glanced around, like she was just now noticing folks lingering to watch. A flush stained her cheeks.

Why hadn't she told this Nelson character to go away?

Nelson watched the interplay between them, then stepped to her side. "I don't believe Elsie's mentioned you in her letters."

In her letters.

Plural. Elsie had been writing this guy. Her intended.

She'd kept it from Nick. The old hurt resurfaced, made him question everything.

Nick had made a mistake coming here. If Elsie was going to refuse her intended, she would've already done it. Clearly, there was someone unwanted here. And it wasn't Nelson.

Nick needed to get out of here.

He was turning on his heel when she snapped, "Excuse me, Arnold."

Nick stalked down the boardwalk, bitterness rising along with the pounding of his pulse in his ears.

"Nick, wait!" Her boots thumped against the boardwalk, running toward him.

He'd passed Mr. Thomas sweeping the rug in front of his shop when Elsie tugged his arm.

"Nick, please!"

He let her tug him to a stop, faced her even as his heart clamored behind his ribs. "Something you forgot to tell me?"

She flinched at the vitriol in his voice.

She glanced at Mr. Thomas, who was clearly listening. Nick didn't care. She'd stopped him, so they could have this conversation now.

"It's not what it looks like." Her mouth trembled as she panted out the words.

He glanced beyond her toward Nelson, still standing where she'd left him, watching.

"He was holding your hands, Elsie. He has a ring." He hadn't meant for her to hear the hurt. *And you didn't tell him to go away.*

She reached for Nick, but he jerked away, and she hugged her waist instead.

"Arnold has been a friend for a long time," she rushed to say. "It's not serious between us."

Guilt shadowed her face. She wasn't telling the whole truth.

"When a fellow offers a ring, Elsie, it's serious."

Her eyes slid closed, releasing tears to cascade down her cheeks. "My parents introduced us. I should've said no when he asked to write me. My mother—"

He knew how her mother used guilt as a weapon, manipulated Elsie's emotions. But even so, Nick found himself asking, "Why didn't you tell your mother you wanted something different? Why not tell him to stop writing, if you didn't want him?"

He knew he was being unreasonable.

"Why didn't you tell me you'd sent off for a mail-order bride?" Her eyes flashed, hurt clear in her words.

Her breath shuddered as she went on. "You don't know what it's like to be an orphan, Nick. To be worried every day that you'll say the wrong thing or do the wrong thing and be sent away."

She drew a shaky breath, and he felt a pang for that little girl Elsie had once been.

"If I tell my mother I won't see Arnold, she won't—"

Love me anymore.

She didn't have to say the words for him to understand. His heart sank. Because where did that leave him?

"So you'll marry him, then?" he asked bitterly. "Just because your mother wants it?"

How could he blame her? Mr. Fancy Suit could provide for her much better than Nick, a failed schoolteacher, could. Ranching was difficult work. Some seasons offered no return.

The fact that she'd led Nick on, let him believe there was a future for them, hurt more than anything.

Still, he had to ask. Give her one last chance to choose him. "Are you going to tell him no?"

She opened her mouth, but no words came out. And her silence shattered Nick's heart.

"I wish you had stayed forgotten."

He turned and strode away.

Seventeen

JUST BEFORE DUSK, THE BLACKENED RUINS of the bunkhouse came into view as Nick rode onto McGraw land. It looked how Nick felt hours after riding away from town. Gutted. Nothing left but an empty shell.

He reined Surrey in a wide circle around the debris to continue toward his cabin.

Earlier that morning, when Nick passed the bunkhouse on his way to town, he'd believed the shambles represented a beacon of hope. A Christmas sign of moving on, past the regrets holding him in place.

Now the heaps of ash looked like another mistake his brothers would have to clean up.

There was no Christmas joy. All that lay ahead for Nick was the isolation of the winter cabin.

The deal was done. He'd filed the paperwork that afternoon. Right after Elsie had shredded his heart.

The deed bulged in his coat pocket. Next to the application he had filled out last night to return to normal school. This morning, he'd thought he'd drop it in the mail. Now he realized the application had been a waste of time.

He was a rancher, pure and simple. One with responsibilities to his family that rolled ahead of him in an endless cycle. Spring and fall. Calving and roundup.

He couldn't face the idea of finding a wife, like he'd asked Merritt to help him with. The only woman he'd ever loved, the only woman he'd ever wanted, was Elsie.

And she didn't love him enough to choose him.

The cutting wind numbed away the sickness in his gut as he stabled his horse in his rustic lean-to and trudged to his cabin.

The squeak of the door's hinges echoed against the cabin's empty walls. It seemed so hollow compared to Drew's home. Only a bed and simple dresser and table. No family. No laughter. No Christmas decorations.

Memories of decorating the big house with Elsie assaulted his brain. The way she'd shown Tillie how to make cornhusk angels and helped Jo with the bows. Sung. Laughed.

He pressed his palm to his throbbing forehead.

Forget.

He couldn't. Not without something to keep him busy. He struck a match, casting a flickering light along the walls.

His gaze snagged on the stores for the winter cabin, stacked against the front wall. Crates of tinned beans, bags of flour, salt, all ready to sustain him until spring.

Someone—Drew?—had pulled the empty wagon outside yesterday.

All that was left for Nick to do was load it up and fulfill what duty required of him.

He hadn't planned on leaving until after Christmas. But the idea of celebrating tomorrow morning felt suffocating.

The kids would be wild with joy. And he'd think of Elsie. Tillie would ask questions about where Elsie was. His big brothers would hover.

He couldn't do it.

Why not leave for the cabin tonight? The majority of the supplies were ready. If he needed more supplies, he could simply snowshoe down from the isolated winter cabin and bring them on a sled.

Before he could change his mind, he went out and hitched Surrey to the wagon.

The sun had almost disappeared below the horizon as Nick carried out the first crate of beans. Patch trailed behind him.

Crate after crate, blood pumping, he carried them out to the wagon, filling the bed.

With only a couple of loads left, he stepped outside, two large bags of flour in his arms.

"What're you doing?" Isaac asked, startling Nick.

Just behind him, Isaac stood, his horse tethered to a post. Nick hadn't even heard his brother ride up.

Isaac crossed his arms. "Thought you weren't heading out until after Christmas."

Nick ignored him. Or at least tried to, but Isaac blocked his path to the back of the wagon. "We didn't see you ride through. Everyone's waiting over at the main house."

Nick shoved the bags into Isaac's chest. "What for?"

With a grunt, Isaac caught the bags before they fell. Nick spun around and headed for the next load.

Behind him, Isaac called, "Wanted to know how things went with—"

Nick slammed the door before Isaac spoke Elsie's name.

Why did his brothers have to be so nosy?

He heaved the last load in his arms, an ache penetrating his shoulder. He'd healed up over the past few days. Had he overdone it with the loading?

Isaac waited, leaning against the wagon. Bothering Nick. "It went that good, huh?"

Nick wanted to slug him, but he chucked the final crate into the back of the wagon instead. Ignoring his brother's scowl, he turned toward his cabin. He only needed to grab his satchel, then he'd be out of there.

"Hey. Slow down." The gruffness of Isaac's tone cut through the frigid air. Nick charged ahead, but Isaac grabbed his arm.

Jerking his arm free, Nick whipped around.

"What happened?" Isaac demanded.

Nick knew his brother wouldn't give up. "She's engaged." Saying the words aloud provided a punch of pain.

Isaac's brows pinched together. "Come again?"

Nick put his hands on his knees to keep from keeling over, his breath coming out in streams of fog from his mouth. "Yep, she's engaged. I surprised them right in the middle of the city slicker's proposal."

Isaac put his hands to his hips. "But she looked at you like you hung the stars. Did you misunderstand something?"

Frustration surged, and Nick pushed off his knees to

stand straight. "Yes, Isaac, because a man holding her hand while offering a wedding band might be asking for directions."

Isaac scratched his beard, his eyes contemplative. "Something ain't right. She loves you. Everyone here could see it. Even Clare mentioned it."

A memory of Elsie standing on the boardwalk, eyes pleading with Nick to understand, flitted through his mind. That was the problem. He did understand. He knew the little girl she'd once been. The young woman who'd only wanted to belong in her adoptive family, to be accepted. If marrying Nelson would truly make her happy, Nick wouldn't stand in her way. How could he? She'd wanted one thing ever since she was a little girl.

Nick shook his head. It wasn't his place to share about Elsie's troubles with her ma. Elsie hadn't chosen him five years ago, and she wasn't choosing him now.

Nick walked into the cabin.

He closed the door, then stuffed a spare shirt and long johns into his satchel. He wouldn't need much else.

He reached for his copy of *Around the World in Eighty Days* but stopped.

He didn't need that either.

He went back outside, whistling for Patch.

Isaac took one look at Nick's satchel and chased after Nick toward the wagon. "Whoa. We're not done talking."

Nick tossed his satchel in. "I'm done." At his signal, Patch bounded into the wagon bed.

"Nick . . ."

Before Isaac could say anything else, Nick climbed up to the buckboard seat. "Tell the others I love them."

With a snap of his reins, Surrey started across the pasture. The rising moon illuminated his path toward the winter cabin.

Hours had passed since Elsie had watched Nick walk away from her.

Again.

Twilight fell outside the window of her classroom, casting shadows over the room. She should head home. The deputy that Marshal O'Grady had assigned to walk her home had checked on her twice already.

Instead, she sat at her desk, gazing at the empty chairs pushed against the walls to make room for the Christmas social tomorrow night, the decorations only half done. The same way Merritt had left it when Elsie had asked to be alone.

Her tears had dried up long ago, and yet Elsie could still feel their salty residue on her cheeks.

After Nick had left, Arnold had come to stand beside her on the boardwalk. She hadn't explained. Only asked him to walk her back to the schoolhouse. He'd seemed to understand that she needed time.

The pine boughs remained draped over the chairs, not yet hung, but their aroma reminded her of what she should be doing.

In her hand, she held the sweet little note written in clumsy pencil left on her desk before break.

Miss Achson, you the best teachr I evr had.

Signed, Wyn. The kindergartner who sat in the front row. The one who Timothy, second grade, pestered constantly by pulling her braids. The one who struggled with spelling but was very quick with arithmetic.

The ache swelled and captured Elsie's breath. Wyn would forget about Elsie before long.

Elsie smoothed her thumb over Wyn's rendition of Miss Atchison. She would have to leave little Wyn. She'd have to leave all of them. With Nick in the area, she couldn't stay here. He'd walked away with such finality resonating in his boot steps that she knew he'd never forgive her.

He'd look for a wife again. Maybe ask Merritt to continue finding him a mail-order bride. Staying in Calvin and watching a wife on his arm would kill Elsie's heart completely.

She had no choice. She'd leave Calvin and find another teaching post.

A knock sounded on the door. Arnold let himself in, still looking fine in his tailored suit. He wasn't smiling this time.

Elsie stood. She could only hope her eyes weren't as red as they felt.

He stayed by the door, as if waiting for an invitation to come closer. "I wanted to check on you."

She took a deep breath. "I owe you some answers."

He glanced down at his hat in his hand, then back up, his expression kind. "The only one I really need is a yes to my proposal."

He stayed in the doorway but kept watching her with an intent look. "Elsie, you're special. Maybe I took too long to express how deep my feelings run, or maybe I didn't say it with eloquent words, but . . ." He sucked in a long breath. "The truth is, I don't care about some cowboy or what must've passed between you. I want to marry you. Take care of you."

Her inhale wobbled.

They were the right words, only . . . the wrong man.

Truth welled inside, and she couldn't contain it any longer. "Nick isn't some cowboy. Not to me. He's so much more than that."

The bare truth in the words resonated. She'd been so worried about hurting Arnold, making things worse, but with that first truth out, the rest of it came more easily.

"I knew Nick in college. We were . . . we were sweethearts, but we parted ways." The words tumbled out like they'd been held back for too long.

Arnold listened.

"I never thought I would see him again, but his family's ranch is here in Calvin—" She cut herself off before she revealed the days they'd been stranded together. Those memories were special. They were hers alone. "Spending time together made me realize I . . . I . . ." She inhaled. "I still love him."

The impact of her words left her trembling. She clenched her hands to her stomach. She hadn't even admitted it to herself until this moment.

She loved Nick. And she'd hurt him by not being able to instantly refuse Arnold, by keeping secrets. How could she ask him to forgive her when she'd done so much damage?

Arnold didn't seem angry. Only contemplative. "I don't

believe that I mistook your affection for me. Not over the several months we corresponded."

Elsie pressed her palms onto her desk. This was part of why she liked Arnold so much as a friend. He wasn't afraid to argue for what he wanted, but he was gentle and kind about it. "I care for you, but not like a wife should. I think of you as a dear friend."

It had never been more obvious than in those moments on the boardwalk. She hadn't thought of Arnold once after Nick's arrival. Her entire focus had been on Nick.

One corner of his mouth pulled in a chagrined smile. He closed the space between them. "I was hoping to hear something different. But, Elsie, friendship can be a great foundation for a marriage to be built on."

Tears burned the back of her eyes again. She wanted more. She wanted love. "A friendship isn't enough to sustain a marriage. Besides I . . . I want to continue teaching." A choked laugh that sounded almost like a sob released from her throat. "I love everything about it."

Arnold tapped his fingers on the nearest desk, thinking. "Your students will always grow up and leave you," he said quietly. "A family—children of your own—is something I know you want."

His words sent a pang through her. Only days ago, she'd dreamed of that. Being Nick's wife. A family of her own. Finding a way to teach, even if she was married. She'd been foolish to dream that she could have both Nick and the job that she loved so dearly. Things didn't work like that.

Arnold was a good friend. He knew the things she wanted. She just didn't want those things with him.

"Just promise me you'll think about it," he said quickly, before she could refuse him a second time. "Give me a chance to win your heart."

He set the ring on the nearby desk, then walked away, leaving her more confused than ever.

Eighteen

T HE NEXT MORNING, NICK TRIED NOT to think about anything at all. He shoved his arms through his coat, getting ready to go check the cattle. On Christmas morning. The job his family needed him to do.

He'd slept for only a few restless hours after he'd arrived late at night, the cabin cold and empty.

Now, the sun brimmed over the horizon, its light spilling through the winter cabin's window. The single room with only a stove, a bed, and a chair, was bathed in the red glow of dawn.

The morning chill bit his skin, and he shivered. He banked the fire in the little stove so it'd be ready for him after a long day in the saddle.

Patch had been glued to Nick's side since last night, watching his every move. Nick patted his head. "Ready to go count head?"

As he straightened, paper in Nick's pocket crinkled.

He pulled out the folded stack of land papers.

He should probably do something with the deed before going out. He couldn't risk damaging it. But as he pulled it out of his pocket, he stilled. Beneath the land papers was another paper.

He unfolded his application for teaching school. What-might-have-beens tore at his throat.

It was time to let go. Time to press forward and stop chasing rainbows. Pa had been right all those years ago.

Clenching his molars so tight they hurt, he swung open the iron stove's door. The application in his fingers trembled, then he flung it in the fire.

Before emotions got the better of him, he turned toward his bed to safely store the land papers in his knapsack.

But as he reached beneath his bed, his hand brushed against a wooden crate.

What was this?

With a furrowed brow, he slid out a crate, but it didn't contain his personal items. Instead, it contained piles and piles of books.

How had these gotten here?

He blinked hard, his head starting to pound. They were the books from when he and Ed had stayed up here several years ago. After his father had passed and they'd gained permission to run cattle on this land. Back when he'd still had dreams.

He hesitated before picking up one of the books.

McGuffey's Fourth Eclectic Reader. He ran his hand over the spine. He'd been the only one in his class to be in the fourth reader. Most of his classmates had only made it to the second.

He opened to the title page, its script familiar.

He'd been so proud back then. What good had it amounted to?

He flipped a page. Then another.

Look how his studying had wounded his family. If not for him, his father would be with them now, wouldn't have lived his last couple of years with a bum leg that hadn't healed right.

He flipped through the book faster, his blood strumming through his ears. If he hadn't been so wrapped up in himself, in his dreams, his ambition . . .

He gripped the corner of the page and ripped it out. He crumpled the paper into a ball in his hand.

He was tired of being the failure.

He balled the page tighter, swiveling toward the stove. He opened the iron door and tossed the page in.

It shriveled, the flames charring it from the outside in.

He ripped out another section, crumpled it and tossed it into the flames.

Then another, then another, momentum propelling him faster. His breath came in gasps, but he kept going.

The front door banged open, and a gust of cold air rushed in.

His brothers traipsed into the small room, bringing snow in on their boots and coats.

Isaac scowled, coming to stand over where Nick squatted in front of the stove. "What are you doing?"

Ed lay down on the bed, boots hanging off the end.

Nick's stare flicked from brother to brother. "Wintering the cattle. What are you doing up here?"

Leaning against the closed door, Drew folded his arms. "We came to talk."

If a lecture was on his brother's mind, Drew had wasted a trip.

"Nothing to talk about," Nick mumbled.

Pity creased Ed's expression, and Nick averted his eyes. He ducked his head and stripped away another section of the book, tossing it into the stove.

"Stop that," Drew growled.

Nick ignored him. "Why? I don't need the books. I'm a rancher. Go back to your families. Have a happy Christmas morning."

"Happy?" Drew asked. "You think we're happy seeing you like this?"

Ed blew out a long breath. "What about school, Nick?"

Another punch of pain. Nick threw another bundle of pages into the fire. "What about it?"

"Tillie said you wanted to go back. Something about an application."

Nick chucked the book binding into the fire. Sparks scattered up the flue. "That was a stupid idea. I'm not going back."

Long silence. He didn't have to look up to know his brothers were exchanging looks.

"I told them about Elsie." Isaac spoke for the first time.

Furious now, Nick's eyes swung to meet Isaac's gaze. He stood against the far wall, arms folded.

Nick picked up another book from the crate, not even reading the cover. "So what?"

"So you go after her." *Dummy.* Ed's insult was implied.

"It's over," Nick said. "Some fancy-pants city slicker came to marry her."

Drew narrowed his eyes. "Were they standing in front of a preacher?"

"What?" Nick's hand paused in the midst of gripping new pages to tear. "No. You don't propose in front of a preacher. That's what the wedding is for."

Ed waved one hand from the bed. "It ain't official until they're in front of a preacher."

Didn't his brothers get it? Elsie had chosen someone else.

"I didn't figure you for someone who gave up so easily," Drew said.

Nick slammed the book cover closed and tossed it back on the crate. "Look, she chose some other guy and made a fool out of me. Just more proof that I'm the weak link—I'll never live up to the rest of you."

All three brothers went quiet. Ed sat up, staring at Nick now.

Isaac gave Nick a pointed look. "What are you talking about?"

Nick ran a hand down his face. He wanted this conversation over so he could do what needed to be done. And be left alone.

He turned his attention back to the stove. "That's what Pa said. Don't you remember?"

The brothers' stares pricked Nick's neck. All remained silent.

Nick's stomach knotted. "That's what Pa called me when I messed up. Weak link." He blinked away the burning behind his nose. "It's why Pa broke his leg and eventually died."

Compassion lit Isaac's expression as Drew and Ed glanced at each other.

Drew palmed the back of his neck. "Nick, you weren't meant to carry that weight. What happened to Pa was an accident."

"But if I hadn't—"

"You have to forgive yourself, Nick." Drew's eyes bored into Nick's, a reflection of the past within their sheen. "We've all made bad decisions, and we've all paid for them."

Nick worked his jaw back and forth. "I'm not like the three of you."

Ed narrowed his gaze, fervor within its depths. "Doesn't make you any less our brother."

Ed's words slammed into Nick's chest. How had Ed pinpointed Nick's fear? That somehow, because of his uniqueness, he didn't belong in this family.

That God had made a mistake when Nick had been born.

Drew pointed a finger straight at Nick. "This family needs you to be who God created you to be. Not some hired hand."

Isaac frowned. "If it hadn't been for your quick thinking and setting fire to the bunkhouse last week, this family would've been devastated."

Drew cleared his throat. "When I think of how I almost lost Kaitlyn, the kids, the baby—"

Ed placed his palm on Nick's shoulder. "Nick, you aren't a weak link. You are a vital link in this family's chain."

"And we don't want you to give up on your own dreams," Drew said.

Isaac thumped Nick in the chest with the back of his hand. "Send in that application."

Nick didn't know what to think. "What about the ranch? Ed's only here half time. Isaac's going back to the Marshals."

Drew looked to Ed and Isaac. "It'll work out. The kids are getting older."

Isaac smirked. "McGraws don't give up."

"Which brings us back to why you've given up on Elsie," Ed said.

"You deserve love too, Nick," Drew said.

"Did you even give her a chance to choose you?" Isaac said.

Nick hadn't. He'd been hurt, humiliated, and had walked away before she could send him away.

"Maybe she wants someone to fight for her," Ed added.

Drew stood straighter. "You're a McGraw, Nick. We fight for what we want. Now, go and get your woman."

Nick could picture the vulnerability and pleading on Elsie's face. She'd claimed she hadn't expected that proposal. But Nick knew her mother wanted her to marry Nelson. Her mother had been helping direct Elsie's life for a long time.

He could so easily picture the little girl trying to win her adoptive parents' love, never wanting confrontation.

She'd been rejected by her own father. Had Nick really

done any different? Rejecting her before she had a chance to break his heart? To protect himself?

She deserved better than that.

Different words from his father rose up from the mist of his memory. *Sometimes, son, you need to stop thinking and get the job done.*

He'd done enough thinking. This time, Pa was right.

Elsie's boot heels clicked on the boardwalk at a meandering pace. Merritt hooked her arm through Elsie's, prompting her to walk faster. "You can't leave things unresolved between you and Arnold. If you don't hurry, we'll miss the train entirely."

It had been Arnold who had insisted she meet him at the train station before he departed. To give him her answer.

An answer she'd begun to question herself.

She'd lain awake all night, thinking from every angle.

The crimson sunset reflected off the remaining snow berms piled in the alleyways, while the air twinged with the stagnant mud on the streets.

Elsie scanned the storefronts of the town she'd come to love, decked out in swags of pine garland and bright bows.

Even on Christmas Day, the boardwalk bustled with townspeople visiting loved ones and delivering gifts, each breath puffing out of their mouths in little white clouds.

Calvin had become home, yet Elsie didn't know how she could stay after all that had happened.

They passed a shadowy back alley, and Elsie's nape prickled with goosebumps.

Danna still hadn't found Quade. Speculated that he'd left town for good. She'd said she believed Elsie to be safe.

So how long would it be before Elsie stopped jumping at every shadow?

The train whistle pierced the night air, and its trill jerked her back to her mission.

Merritt slanted a glance toward Elsie. "Would it be so bad if your answer to Arnold were yes?"

Whose side was Merritt on? Nick was her cousin.

The ring Arnold had proposed with hung on a string around Elsie's neck, hidden beneath her dress.

She couldn't wear it.

"Merry Christmas, Miss Atchison." Rory, one of her students, waved furiously from the back of a wagon parked across the street.

She waved back, her heart aching.

She couldn't walk away from her students. Could she? Even if it meant seeing Nick in town.

She just didn't know what to do.

Merritt sighed. "Elsie, what do *you* want?"

It was just like Merritt to cut to the heart of the matter. "Is it so wrong to want a family of my own? Someone who'll care about me? Arnold is offering me that."

"Of course not." Compassion warmed Merritt's voice. "I wanted it, and God brought me Jack."

Merritt strolled a few more steps, quiet. "Do you still want those things with a man who isn't Nick?"

Elsie's muddled feelings were all Nick's fault. Being on the ranch had let her see how the McGraws loved each other. With all their faults and failures, no family could be more loyal. Elsie wanted to belong to a family like that.

Merritt tugged Elsie to a stop on the street in front of the train station. "Will you really be happy if you say yes because it's what your mother wants?"

Elsie squeezed her eyes closed. "She'll be so angry if I reject Arnold. Stay in bed for weeks." She ducked her head as her deepest fear blurted from her lips. "What if she says I'm not her daughter any longer?"

Her father had abandoned her. Never given a reason. Just stopped loving her.

What had Elsie done so wrong to make him give her away to a distant cousin who didn't want her either?

The question always churned inside, never finding an answer.

Merritt's hand closed around Elsie's, a gesture of comfort that let Elsie draw air into a tight chest.

"She didn't stop loving you when you cut your hair off at fourteen. Or when you moved to Calvin, even though she wanted you close." Merritt's eyes became earnest. "Elsie, even if your mother stops, I love you. Darcy loves you. Nick loves you."

A sob hiccupped out as Elsie started to shake her head. Nick didn't love her. But Merritt squeezed her hand.

"God loves you. Enough to adopt you as *His* daughter. You are a child of the King. Isn't it time you started loving yourself?"

Something about Merritt's words shattered a wall around Elsie's heart.

Adopted by a heavenly Father. The idea seemed too

grand to be true, yet warmth wrapped around her, so tender, so comforting that it couldn't be anything but true.

Elsie drew in a cleansing breath and pinched her eyes closed, releasing tears to stream down her face.

To simply be who she was created to be, to stop trying to earn her way—it tore away the burden weighing on her heart.

Merritt pushed a kerchief into her hand. "Do you really think that marrying Arnold is the right thing?" Merritt whispered.

No.

The word echoed within her heart like a church bell heard for miles around. She couldn't marry Arnold.

Elsie reached for the string around her neck and pulled the ring loose. Merritt watched, tense. Waiting for Elsie's decision.

Elsie sighed. "I think I need to go give Arnold his ring back."

Merritt smiled. "I think maybe you do."

Elsie bit her lip and glanced toward the train's steam, expanding into the frigid air above the building. "This is going to be hard."

Merritt wrapped her in a tight hug. "But you can do it."

The train whistle blew its last warning.

Merritt pushed her toward the platform. "Go! I'll wait right here."

Elsie picked up her skirts and rushed up the steps to the platform.

"Elsie!"

Glancing up, Elsie found Arnold leaning out the window

of the second to last car. He waved, then motioned toward the door.

Swallowing the lump in her throat, Elsie hurried to meet him.

Arnold met her at the door to the car, leaning down. "I didn't think you were going to make it."

The conductor shouted from behind her. "All aboard!"

Elsie opened her sweaty palm and held out the ring. "I'm sorry, Arnold. I can't marry you."

Arnold looked resigned. "So, that's it, then?"

Elsie hoped Arnold could read the apology in her eyes. "It is."

He closed his hand around the ring. The peace she'd been waiting for, hoping for, flooded her core.

Bending down, he kissed her cheek. "I wish you the best. You'll make that rancher very happy."

If Nick forgave her. If she wasn't too late.

Her mouth tipped into a smile. "He's not a rancher. He's a teacher."

The train jolted, the engine steam hissing in the air. Elsie stepped away as Arnold backed into the car.

He waved. "Good luck."

A final blast of the whistle rang in Elsie's ears as the train chugged forward.

She turned, determined to meet Merritt, then find Rebekah and a way back to the ranch. She'd only taken one step when an arm snaked around her torso from behind and a hand clamped over her mouth.

Elsie struggled, but the big, strong man held fast, looming over her.

The platform had already begun to clear, and no one seemed to notice as he dragged her into the shadows on the far end.

Where was he taking her? The platform ended—

He threw himself back, dragging her along with him off the edge of the platform. Elsie plummeted into darkness.

Nineteen

EVENING SHADOWS WERE GROWING long over the streets as Nick rode into Calvin. Urgency pulsed through him to speak to Elsie. To apologize. To tell her he'd been a fool.

And, hopefully, not make a bigger fool of himself when he asked her to choose him over the man with the fancy suit and silver ring.

It was getting colder. The slushy mud beneath his horse's hooves was already beginning to freeze.

He was heading to Merritt's to ask for Elsie's whereabouts, but a familiar figure caught his eye near the train platform

The train whistle shrilled as he approached.

Steam from the engine billowed into the air over the platform.

"Everything quiet, Merritt?" he asked. He'd heard Danna still hadn't captured Quade.

Merritt studied him. "Is all well at the ranch? I wasn't expecting you in town."

His breath hitched. He was doing the right thing, but a sudden shot of nerves nipped at his stomach. "Fine. I need to speak with Elsie."

The corners of her mouth tipped into a knowing smile. "It's about time. She hopped on the train—"

The whistle blew again, cutting off her words. His horse pranced beneath him.

If Elsie was on the train, did that mean she'd gotten engaged?

Not in front of the preacher.

Drew's words ran through his mind. He'd come this far—he wasn't giving up. He hopped off Surrey and tossed the reins to Merritt. "Can you tie him up?"

He didn't wait for her answer but took the steps to the platform two at a time.

The train whistle signaled its final shrill.

A few stragglers got on the train, and several folks were headed off away from it. He was striding toward the nearest door to hop on when he caught sight of a familiar shock of blonde hair.

Elsie.

Standing on the platform. Not on the train. Her beau leaned down and kissed her cheek, and Nick's gut twisted—but the man waved and left her on the platform as the train chugged away.

Determination rose and he took a deep breath. *Don't give up.*

He started toward her, but before he could call her name, a shadowy figure looped his arm around Elsie from behind.

Nick stiffened. Who . . .

Passing light fell from the window of the last car, flashing over the man's face.

Quade.

Nick's gut seized.

"Get help!" he shouted to the station attendant.

His legs pumped as he tore across the platform.

Quade dragged Elsie off the platform.

No!

Nick followed close enough to see they'd jumped into an empty freighter wagon.

He stumbled to a stop at the edge of the platform. Inside the wagon, Quade held Elsie in front of him, a revolver against her heart.

Tears sparkled on Elsie's lashes. She looked like she was holding her breath.

Raw anger twisted inside Nick.

Quade stared at him, silently daring Nick to do something.

He was barely recognizable. His usually impeccable suit was rumpled. His stained hat—askew. His face lined. But it was his eyes that frightened Nick. A look that said only one of them was going to live through this.

Nick quickly vowed that he would do whatever it took to save Elsie.

Quade's glare skittered toward a noise from nearby—

Nick surged from the platform toward the wagon. He collided into Quade, and his momentum knocked both of them out of the wagon bed. They landed on the muddy ground with a thud that jarred Nick's shoulder so painfully he saw stars.

"Nick!" Elsie's shout was muffled. She was still in the wagon bed. "Help!"

Nick grappled with Quade. In the dark of the evening, he couldn't see. Where was the gun?

It blasted from so close that Nick's ears rang.

Something hot grazed the outside of his arm.

Fury fueling his strength, Nick clutched both hands around Quade's gun arm. He had to get that gun before Quade had a chance to turn it on Elsie.

Nick threw his elbow into Quade's face and heard a satisfying crunch.

Quade pressed his thumb into the bullet wound in Nick's arm. The sudden flare of white-hot pain rendered his arm useless, and Quade rolled on top of Nick, one arm now across Nick's neck, cutting off his air supply.

"You McGraws have stolen everything from me." Spittle flew from Quade's mouth. The lethal tone of his voice sent a shiver down Nick's spine.

"Stop!"

Somewhere in the background was the sound of rustling and shouts.

A thump. Like someone had fallen from a wagon. Or jumped.

Quade looked up. Elsie was in danger.

A sneer twisted Quade's face. "Now it's my turn to take everything from you."

He yanked his arm from Nick's grip, raised the gun, and fired. The bullet flew wild into the night sky.

In the distance, someone shouted.

Nick bucked, dislodging Quade from on top of him.

"Nick!" Elsie cried.

Quade backhanded him in the jaw with the gun.

Spots danced before Nick's eyes. He shook his head, tried to focus.

Elsie was standing right there. Too close.

Quade took aim.

Nick used the last of his strength to throw himself at Quade. He collided as the gun fired again, pulling Quade to the ground.

Ears ringing, he couldn't tell where the shot had hit. Quade used the beat of uncertainty to pin Nick, kneeling on top of him.

Out of the blackness, a force collided into Quade, tackling him off Nick. "Get back," the man shouted.

Nick lay on the ground, struggling to breathe.

Off to the side, Quade struggled with the man as Nick shoved up on his elbows, intending to go help contain Quade.

Another man appeared, this one with a star pinned to his chest.

Jack.

He drew his revolver and pointed it at Quade, who went still.

Light bobbed. Someone was bringing a lantern.

Quade surrendered his weapon, and as the light got

brighter, several bystanders gathered on the nearest corner of the platform.

Still breathing hard, pain pulsing in two different places on his shoulder, Nick sat up on the frozen ground.

"Nick!" Elsie was beside him in a billow of skirts.

The sound of her voice sent prickles over his skin.

His gaze swept over her, looking for any blood or signs of injury. "Did he hurt you?"

Tears tracked down her cheeks as she shook her head. "I'm fine."

He closed his eyes as a wave of dizziness hit. He steadied himself with one hand on the ground. Elsie was unharmed.

Relief pulsed through him. He heard Quade's voice and forced his eyes open. Quade was blabbering nonsense as he was dragged away by Chas O'Grady and another deputy. Jack remained behind, talking to one of the townspeople. Jack caught Nick's eye and nodded.

It was over.

And suddenly Nick's heart was pounding for another reason. Had Elsie agreed to marry her city-slicker beau?

Nick wanted to reach for her, fold her in his arms, but he wasn't sure he had the right.

"You're hurt." Elsie's teeth chattered as she knelt next to Nick in the cold mud.

He'd clamped one hand over his upper arm, and there was a trickle of blood at the corner of his mouth.

She felt the intensity of his gaze as she pulled his hand

away. His upper sleeve was soaked in blood, and she pressed her hand there to staunch the flow. Nick hissed in pain.

Merritt ran up, carrying a lantern. Her expression tightened as she knelt at Nick's other side. "How is he?"

In the improved light, Elsie could see the bruise blooming on his jaw, the set of his mouth that meant he was holding back. There had been three or four shots. Was he hit somewhere else?

"Bleeding everywhere," she told Merritt tightly.

Merritt scanned the onlookers. "We need a doctor!"

Nick cupped Elsie's elbow with his free hand. "The bullet only grazed me."

He sounded calm and sure. Not confused and weak like before at the doctor's office.

Merritt's gaze took in Nick from the top of his head to the bottom of his boots. "Are you sure?"

"I can walk to the doctor on my own. Just give me a minute." His eyes returned to Elsie.

The certainty in his words and Merritt's nod—she believed him too—made everything Elsie was feeling from the last few minutes bubble over. Tears spilled over, and a tiny sob escaped.

Nick was already reaching for her when she did what she really wanted to do and pressed close, putting one arm around his neck.

Merritt faded back. "Jack is beckoning me. Probably wants to know what I saw. I'll be right back."

She'd come so close to losing him. Again.

Nick cupped the back of her head with one hand. "Oh, El, don't cry."

His words only made her cry harder. He pressed his jaw into the top of her hair.

He'd protected her, put himself in front of that bullet. *For her.*

The night could have gone very differently, and the realization weighed upon her like a heap of stones.

She had so much to say, but words jumbled around in her head.

"I'm all right," he whispered. "They got Quade. It's safe now. No more looking over your shoulder." It was as if he knew everything she needed to hear in this moment. "In a few days, you'll be back in your schoolroom. Everything will be back to normal."

It was the hesitation before his last words that had her pushing back to look at his face. She wiped tears from her cheeks. Saw the uncertainty in his expression.

He reached up to tuck a lock of hair behind her ear. His hand faltered. "You've got a scrape." Nick's lips flattened. "I should've hit him harder."

She glanced at where she'd seen her attacker being carted away. "No, the law has him. It's over now."

There was a release in the words.

It really was over. Quade had been arrested. There were witnesses. Charges would stick. The McGraws could finally have peace.

Nick's breath teased her cheeks. Had he leaned closer?

"El . . ." He traced his thumb along her jaw. "I've got some things to say."

She froze, lowering her eyes. The hurtful words they'd thrown at each other yesterday played in her mind. "Yes?"

He dropped his hand away, looking serious. "I'm sorry for the way I spoke to you yesterday. I should've stayed and talked things out. That was unfair of me."

His apology settled inside her.

And he wasn't the only one to blame. "Can you forgive me as well? I should've told you about my parents' expectations." She swallowed. "And Arnold."

Why had it taken her so long to say her goodbye to him?

Nick's eyes cut away. A muscle jumped in his cheek.

His vulnerability touched Elsie, but—"Why did you come back to town?" she whispered.

His chin jutted out a bit, another sign of vulnerability, and then he looked her right in the eyes. "I don't know if you said yes to Arnold . . ." He paused. "But I love you, and I want you to choose me. Marry me."

His words seeped into every broken place of her heart, healing every piece of her, making her want to laugh and cry all at once.

She wrapped his hand in both of hers, feeling his strength when he clasped his fingers around hers. He really was okay.

He went on. "I know I don't have a lot to offer. Not yet. But I'm going back to the normal school and—"

"You are? Oh, Nick!" Elsie couldn't contain her surge of happiness as she threw her arms around his neck.

He chuckled into her hair, his uninjured arm coming around her waist.

Someone cleared their throat nearby.

Marshal O'Grady was staring down at them. Along with several curious townspeople behind her. Merritt stood off to the side, her mouth quirked into a smile.

Elsie drew back slightly but stayed kneeling next to Nick. Her cheeks flushed with heat despite the chilly air.

This was the moment she should be worried about her reputation, but she found she couldn't care.

Nick loved her. A wonderful thing that had once seemed impossible. Now it seemed anything good could happen.

Danna strode to them, all business. "I have some questions about how tonight's events unfolded. Can you come to the office and give your statements?"

Nick started to push himself up off the ground but inhaled sharply. When he wavered, Elsie reached out to support him. "Nick needs the doctor first."

Nick dragged himself to stand. Elsie stuck close to his side.

He whispered, "Bossy."

She couldn't keep from meeting his secret smile with one of her own.

Danna's brows rose. "Visit the doctor, then come see me. Don't get distracted." One corner of her mouth twitched.

Nick grinned. "No guarantees."

Danna tipped the brim of her hat, then headed toward the jail, signaling for the crowd to disperse. Several folks walked off.

Merritt met them at the edge of the boardwalk. "Do you need help? Should I get Ed?"

Nick scoffed. "Bullet barely nicked me."

No, what Elsie needed was time with Nick. A moment with just the two of them. "I can handle it."

Merritt glanced between Elsie and Nick, eyes sparkling. "I guess now's not a good time to tell you I had an answer to one of my letters. A young lady who wants to correspond with Nick."

Nick glanced down at Elsie, his eyes so intense they sent a flutter to her toes. "I'm not interested in answering any letters. Not anymore."

Merritt smiled and walked away, muttering something like "It's about time" beneath her breath.

The silence of the night settled around them as they made their way down the street, Elsie sticking close to Nick, Nick a little slow but sturdy. The shadows no longer felt threatening. Not with Quade captured.

When they made it to the edge of the boardwalk to cross the street, Nick grinned. "Maybe I am feeling woozy. You'd better put your arm around me."

Elsie slid her arm around Nick's waist. "Woozy, huh? We can't have that."

Nick chuckled. "No, darling, we sure can't."

Their footfalls beat along the boardwalk in the quiet of the evening.

It still held her in awe. That he'd been there. That he'd fought for her. "I can't believe you came for me."

Nick leaned a little closer, his breath brushing her cheek. "I'll always come for you." He'd lowered his tone to an affectionate rumble. "I love you."

She looked up into his face, seeing only sincerity. "I love you too, Nick. I always have."

Even when she had believed she'd never see him again, even when he had promised to forget her, she'd loved him.

He pulled her tighter, lowering his lips to her temple. "You're not marrying that other guy."

It wasn't a question, but she answered anyway. "No. I couldn't have gone through with it, not when my heart belongs to you. Even when you didn't want me anymore, it was always yours."

He drifted to a stop and turned her toward him. "Darling, that was jealousy talking. I was acting stupid. Glad my brothers knocked some sense into me."

A snicker escaped from her lips. She could only imagine how that had gone. "I hope they didn't knock you too hard."

He shrugged. "I deserved it."

She laughed again, joy bubbling from her gut.

He drew back until he looked into her face. The light from the nearby building illuminated his knit brow. "You didn't answer my question from earlier." He drew in a breath. "If you'll marry me."

Elsie bit her lip against the grin she couldn't stop. "Technically, you didn't ask."

The roguish smile that always released butterflies into her stomach crossed his mouth. "El." He smoothed her hair behind her ear, stopping to cradle her cheek. "El-Belle, will you marry me?"

Tears of joy she couldn't contain sprang to her eyes. "Yes."

The line of tension in his forehead relaxed. Had he really not known her answer would be yes? It had always been yes, from the moment he'd made her smile beside the Christmas tree all those years ago.

He leaned down, hesitating only a breath before he brushed his lips against hers. His kiss felt like hope. Like home. Like love.

She responded to his kiss, trying to communicate her sincerity. Her devotion. And that she would always stand by him. No matter what.

He shifted to put his arm around her, and when he did, she felt him wince a little.

She pulled away from his eager lips. "Come on. Let's go see the doctor."

He groaned, but she felt his smile against her cheek. "Always so bossy."

She stifled her giggle to sound as serious as possible. "Only to you."

He chuckled. "Merry Christmas, my darling."

She tugged the brim of his hat. "Merry Christmas."

He brushed one more kiss over her lips, then she turned him in the direction of the doctor's office.

As they walked along the boardwalk, comfortable in each other's presence, she didn't know what the future would hold. Whether she'd be allowed to keep teaching after they married, or what would happen with the McGraw land, or even if Quade would be sentenced.

But she did know that Nick would stand beside her through it all.

And that was enough.

Twenty

September 1894 - Nine Months Later

ELSIE LOVED THE SMELL OF A NEW school year. The fresh paper. The chalk. The end of summer breeze through the windows. New beginnings. She was back where she belonged.

She glanced around her classroom, a broom and dustpan in her hand. There. With the floor swept, she only had a few unfinished touches before the first day of school tomorrow.

She rubbed the stiffness away from her neck, her muscles aching. The last few days had been nonstop.

The past nine months had been nonstop.

Starting right after Christmas, when Nick left Calvin to finish his teaching certificate. It'd been harder than she'd expected to say goodbye, to have a long-distance courtship.

Now she picked up the pile of slates on a bookshelf and absently started to lay one on each desk.

Last spring, Nick's graduation couldn't come fast

enough. Knowing Nick would only be gone a few months and that he would come home almost every weekend had helped, but those weekends had been brief, sometimes only allowing a few hours together before he had to take the train back.

She'd been so lonely without him.

But . . .

Oh, the love letters he'd sent would make any girl swoon. Letters that she would cherish forever. She'd written back faithfully.

She shook her head and continued her task. The slate frames tapped on the wooden desks, echoing in the room.

The day of their wedding finally came. Everything had been so wonderful.

May flowers had bloomed, and the aroma of springtime and happiness had flooded the air.

She'd never been so happy—to be united with him and take his name. Nearly everyone in Calvin had attended. Mother and Father had come in on the train.

When she'd written to her mother about Nick, she'd been so worried about how her parents would react to her choice. She'd been nearly sick on the train trip at the end of the Christmas holidays to introduce Nick.

To say they'd been coolly distant was an understatement. But it hadn't rattled Nick at all. No, he'd been calm, confidant, and charming. And the best part—not once had he left her side.

By the end of the weekend, somehow, he'd won them over. Even had them laughing. Of course.

Calvin had also been through some changes in the last few months.

She placed the last slate down and swiped her hands together as she moved to her desk.

In April, Merritt had been elected as the first woman on the school board and became instrumental in the changes the school desperately needed.

One being that the town's population growth required a second classroom.

And a second teacher.

Starting tomorrow, the school would have two teachers. Mr. and Mrs. McGraw.

Elsie suspected Merritt had helped sway the board's vote to allow her to remain teacher, provided she worked alongside her husband.

It was the perfect solution. She'd teach the younger kids and he the older ones. Last night, he'd confessed he was nervous for the first day in the classroom, but she knew he'd be brilliant.

She picked up a stack of readers and carried them to the bookshelf. She arranged them carefully, easiest to hardest.

It had taken most of the summer to build the second classroom next to the first. The construction had finished a few days ago, and they'd spent every hour cleaning and furnishing the two rooms, preparing everything for the kids.

She breathed in deeply, the aroma of the fresh lumber mixing in with the late-summer breeze from the window.

She should probably check and see how her husband was faring.

On her way out of the room, she picked up the broom

and dustpan to take with her. She moved through the newly extended cloakroom and then to the new classroom.

At the threshold, her feet planted to the floorboards. Nick stood at the chalkboard, a piece of chalk poised in his hand, not moving.

He held so still that she didn't want to breathe and disturb him.

The past few days, he'd been hustling around with excitement to start his new position, unable to even sit. So much so that now, the stillness concerned her.

She'd thought Nick was happy. He hadn't stopped smiling. But why was he just standing there at the board?

She moved to go to him, but he raised the chalk to the board. It scraped against the blackboard as he wrote *Mr. McGraw* in perfect penmanship.

Oh.

Writing his name signaled more than helping new students remember his name. It was him taking possession of his classroom.

Elsie bit her lip as tears pricked the backs of her eyes. This was where he should've been all along, and seeing him finally step into his position made her love for him swell inside her.

After everything they'd been through, seeing his name on the board was even more significant.

To keep from startling him, she set the dustpan and broom down as softly as possible.

He heard anyway and glanced over his shoulder. She moved toward him.

A lopsided smile lifted his mouth as he reached for the eraser. "I'm being silly."

"No." Elsie put her hand on his arm to stop him from erasing it. "Leave it. You deserve to savor it. Enjoy it in whatever way you'd like."

A smoldering look came into his eyes as he snagged her toward him. "Whatever way I like, huh. I'd like to enjoy a kiss from my wife."

He lowered his lips toward hers, but Elsie leaned back and bopped her finger against his nose. "You, sir, are an upstanding teacher, a leader in the schoolroom, and an example of good behavior for the entire county. You'd better behave."

He tilted his head, an ornery grin on his face. "Starting tomorrow, perhaps."

He leaned in again, but she pushed against his chest and maneuvered out of his arms. She pointed to the dustpan she'd left on a bench by the back door. "There's still work to be done, Mr. McGraw."

Mr. McGraw. And she was Mrs. McGraw. She'd never tire of saying that.

She weaved through the desks to reach the dustpan, Nick still at the front of the room, a roguish posture in his shoulders.

"I have an idea."

She didn't turn around. She couldn't encourage him.

"We'll make the children clean the room." His footsteps approached her from behind. "Or better yet, bribe them."

She turned on her heel with her fists on her hips. "Really. I can tell who's gunning to be the favorite teacher."

He stepped closer slowly. Intentionally.

Elsie inched back, her hands held out in front of her. "Nick. Stop being such a rascal."

A sly grin appeared on his face, and he drew closer. "A rascal? Since when does kissing my wife make me a rascal?"

He lunged forward to catch her waist, but Elsie evaded the move with a squeal.

He followed her through the desks, his pursuit slow and methodical. Elsie laughed and braced herself behind his teacher desk.

He lurched to the left. When Elsie evaded the other way, he changed direction and caught her skirt in his hand. "Ahha!" He reeled her back to him, but she didn't try to stop him. "I've got you."

Elsie tried to calm her breath. "You sure do." Outside, Patch barked. She smiled bigger. "Just in time for our company."

"Ahhh." When Nick loosened his grip, Elsie slid away. Nick's arms flopped to his sides as he groaned. "Who invited my brothers?"

Elsie picked up a pile of readers on his desk. "You did."

He scratched the back of his head. "I didn't think that through very well."

Boots stepped through the cloakroom and into the classroom, but it wasn't one of Nick's brothers. Instead, it was Mr. Jamison, one of the school board members.

Not her favorite person in the world. Especially when he hadn't been fond of the idea of her retaining her teaching position after marrying Nick.

Patch followed him in, the dog's movements edgy. Elsie knew how he felt.

"Patch, come." When his dog came near, Nick motioned for him to lie down. "Mr. Jamison, how can I help you?"

Mr. Jamison's eyes scanned the room. Elsie didn't miss how the board member's eyes skipped right over her. "Good day, Mr. McGraw."

Nick paused, glancing over at Elsie, but the man didn't even acknowledge her.

She smoothed a loose lock of hair behind her ear and turned toward the bookcase to put the readers in their place.

Mr. Jamison came farther to the room. "It's looking good in here. A very nice classroom indeed. You've done an excellent job making things ready."

Elsie kept her back to them, straightening the bookshelf.

"Thank you, Mr. Jamison, but it wasn't me. It was mostly Elsie."

Elsie's hand hesitated on the book as she twisted toward Nick.

He watched her, softness in his eyes. "She's the one who knows what she's doing. I'm just in training."

Elsie shook her head. Hardly. Teaching came like breathing to Nick.

Mr. Jamison looked at Elsie and nodded toward her. "Oh, yes. Of course."

As Mr. Jamison spoke, Nick didn't take his gaze from her. Like always, he saw deeper than what was on the outside. Deeper than what everyone else saw.

And he wouldn't let anyone overlook her. Or forget her.

Nick dragged his attention back to the board member as he explained some of the changes they'd made. Together.

Elsie folded her hands and listened. A ribbon of joy twined inside, and she drew in a long inhale.

She was truly blessed.

Nick had thought this day would never come. The day he stepped out of his own classroom, prepared for students the next day.

He inhaled all that the summer's late-afternoon breeze brushed over him. The grass. The overtone of fresh paint on the school's clapboard siding. Even Kaitlyn's nearby cherry pie.

All of his brothers and their families had turned out for this celebration picnic. The beginning of the school year.

The children had run in and out of the school, pointing out the new things on the walls. Tillie had stood behind his desk, pointer aimed at the chalkboard, helping her imaginary students recite their ABCs.

He scanned the schoolyard, yearning to set eyes on his beloved. She'd nestled into his family like she'd belonged there all along, but he still wanted to assure himself she was fine.

In the mix of ladies, he found her. And she was more than fine. She carried Kaitlyn's baby in her arms, her cheeks glowing as she whispered something in the baby's ear.

Heat radiated through his chest. She looked even more beautiful with a baby in her arms. Maybe, when it was time, she'd be carrying her own babies. Their babies.

For now, though, he wanted to cherish these days of it being only the two of them. And about thirty-two students.

How much time had he wasted sulking? How much time had he wasted by not forgiving Elsie? By not showing grace and understanding?

No more. He didn't want to miss a thing. Not waking up beside her with the sun glistening off her hair, nor sneaking food off her plate at lunchtime. Nor a kiss while grading papers at the table at night.

Time marched fast enough on its own. He didn't want to hurry it by one second.

He'd been restored. Had finally been able to take the position he'd wanted all along.

From behind, Eli bumped into him, trying to scoot by. "Sorry, Uncle Nick!"

Nick waved him on.

"Perhaps you should stop gawking at your woman and get out of the doorway, little brother," Isaac called out.

Nick shrugged. What could he say? Isaac was right. Elsie was captivating.

His brothers lingered in the shade of the schoolhouse, discussing business. They'd all cleared their chores for the afternoon to come celebrate with Nick. To support him in his new endeavor.

And it warmed him all the way to his core.

They were truly happy for him.

"They're saying Isabella isn't going to sell. She wants to run the ranch."

Ed's words drew Nick's attention as he approached. Nick

hadn't seen Isabella Quade around much since her father had been sentenced to ten years in prison.

Couldn't say he blamed her. He felt bad for the gal caught up in the thick of her father's many mistakes. But he would never feel sorry for Quade.

The trial had been swift. The unexpected testimony of one of Quade's old cowhands about his motives had been the clincher, sending him to prison for attempted murder twice over. Ever since Danna had hauled him away, things had been peaceful for the McGraw family.

He wished he could say the same for Quade's oldest daughter.

Ed leaned against the schoolhouse wall. "Rebekah heard from Mr. Brady at the post office that Isabella had to stop the payments to that fancy boarding school the two youngest attend in St. Louis."

Isaac let out a long whistle. "Think they'll come home? I haven't seen Sophia and Charlotte in years."

Ed shrugged.

Drew twiddled a long piece of grass. "Isabella seems to be trying to make peace with anybody Quade wronged."

Nick had heard that, but it didn't seem to be going well. Some people Quade had wronged had even tried to bring a civil suit. Each suit had been dismissed on lack of evidence, which had only riled the community up more.

Quade had been careful. It didn't matter if he'd bought someone's homestead at a fraction of its value, the papers were legal. He owned it.

No one could prove that he'd bribed or blackmailed

Ernie Duff either. Duff had stepped down as land officer and moved away. Convenient, if you asked Nick.

"Maybe Isabella should sell," Ed said. "She can't wrangle that much land and those cattle on her own."

Drew released a long sigh. "She's always seemed a little like Jo to me. I think she's pretty determined to keep the ranch. It has been her home her whole life."

Isaac grunted in agreement, his attention wandering around the school yard. Always watchful.

"I was out by the north field today, and I think we're going to have a good harvest," Ed said.

Isaac replied with something, but Nick's mind meandered toward Elsie as she passed the baby back to Kaitlyn.

Drew jerked his head, indicating for Nick to follow him. After another glance toward Elsie, he did.

"You've done good for yourself, little brother."

Nick couldn't respond right away.

He'd helped at the ranch through the summer. He and Elsie had stayed in his cabin out there while he'd assisted with the summer's labor. Something they planned on doing next summer too. It gave him a way to contribute to their family's ranch.

However, the remainder of the year, there'd be one less hand on the McGraw ranch, and it still sat wrong in the pit of Nick's stomach.

After a bit, Nick drew in a breath. "As soon as school lets out on breaks, I'll be back to help—"

"Nick." Drew's brow lowered. "You are where you're meant to be. The ranch will be fine. I'm proud of you for chasing your dream. And your woman. Elsie is something else."

Drew didn't need to tell that to Nick. A grin that probably looked goofy spread across his face.

At that moment, Elsie turned and caught him staring. It was a regular occurrence.

She tilted her head, and he forgot to breathe for a moment.

He hoped that reaction would never end.

He found himself moving toward her without really thinking about it, caught in her magnetic pull.

They met in the middle, the family's chaos swirling around them. Her eyes sparkled, and she'd never looked more lovely.

She truly was happy. Even among his crazy, noisy, and nosy family.

She slid her hand into his. "You ready to teach tomorrow?"

A swell of something sweet and wonderful lifted his chest. "You better believe it."

She glanced around the yard. "Your whole family is here. To celebrate you."

The truth rooted in deep. He was a strong link in their family chain. A part of the McGraw legacy.

He hadn't seen it, not with the difficult circumstances and the mistakes he'd made along the way.

He slid his arm around Elsie's waist, his heart full.

God didn't make a mistake. He really did work everything out for good.

Bonus Epilogue

Are you are a member of our new releases newsletter? You can receive a special gift, available only to newsletters subscribers.

This Bonus Epilogue to *A Forgotten Heart* will not be released on any retailer platform—it's only available to newsletter subscribers.

Find out what happens next with Nick and Elsie. Scan this QR code to subscribe and get your free gift. You acknowledge you are becoming a Sunrise Publishing, Traci Summeril and Lacy Williams subscriber. Unsubscribe from any newsletter at any time.

Thank You

Thank you again for reading *A Forgotten Heart*. We hope you enjoyed the story. If you did, would you be willing to do us a favor and leave a review? It doesn't have to be long—just a few words to help other readers know what they're getting. (But no spoilers! We don't want to wreck the fun!) Thank you again for reading!

We'd love to hear from you—not only about this story, but about any characters or stories you'd like to read in the future.

Contact us at www.sunrisepublishing.com/contact.

READ ON FOR MORE FROM THE

Wind River
MAIL-ORDER BRIDES
SERIES

Experience Christmas with our Wind River Mail-Order Brides in a new anthology, Snowbound at Christmas, presented by Lacy Williams with Wendy Galinetti, Wendy Klopfenstein, and Traci Summeril.

One Christmas snowstorm creates havoc for three couples who find themselves snowed in together—and a chance for new love to bloom and old feelings to be rekindled. Curl up on a winter's afternoon with this anthology of three heartwarming love stories set in the Wind River story world.

Heart's Secret Haven

Livery owner Lilly Murdock would prefer to skip over Christmas entirely. She's given up on finding love. What kind of man wants a wife who spends her days tending to the stable and who smells like a horse? When a snowstorm traps her with her childhood friend, old dreams come back to life. Rancher Jakob Anderson can't think of a worse punishment than being stuck inside the barn for days with the woman he once loved and never forgot. As he spends more time with Lilly, he realizes the feelings he thought he'd gotten over are just as strong as ever...

Her Gingerbread Refuge

Widowed bakery owner Caroline Wilson has one wish: to give her children a perfect Christmas. When a stranger and his young sister blow into her small-town bakery in the middle of a blizzard, she finds all her careful plans upended... and finds herself drawn to the driven businessman. Jerome Barnett doesn't know what to do with a younger sister—one he didn't even know existed until a letter arrived. It's Caroline that helps them connect, and Caroline that begins to melt his guarded heart.

Her Yuletide Protector

Heiress Lizzie Hamilton is on a desperate quest to escape an arranged marriage and finds herself trapped on a snowed-in train and mistaken for a common thief. She can't trust anyone, not even the deputy with shadowed eyes and a vulnerability beneath his hard exterior. Deputy Slate Jackson sees everything in black and white. But Lizzie is a conundrum. Kind to small children, afraid of every noise, a sadness she can't seem to shake. Is she really a thief or is she hiding a different kind of secret? When the snow begins to melt and the danger chasing Lizzie draws close, Slate must decide whether he can trust Lizzie... and his own heart.

One

A CHILL SLIPPED DOWN LILLY MUR-dock's collar.

It wouldn't be long now until the blizzard hit. She could feel its icy fingers already gripping the town of Calvin. She grasped the handles of the wheelbarrow heaped with hay and pushed it along the central aisle of the stable. Bandit, a scruffy ranch dog with a patchwork coat of brown, white, and black that some cowboy drifter had left behind, followed on her heels.

The almanac had predicted the snowstorm. Pa would've said he felt it coming in his bones.

She missed his dear voice.

She'd been up at dawn, hauling in bags of feed and filling the water barrels. With eight rental horses to look after and another five boarded for the town's residents, she was "riding with a full saddlebag." Another thing Pa used to say. Lilly took in a deep breath against the familiar tightness in her chest. Almost a year now since Pa passed. It didn't feel right that he was gone. Sometimes she would look up, expecting to find him mucking out a stall or sitting at the table repairing a bridle in their small living quarters.

As she passed by one of the middle stalls, a familiar soft nicker called to her.

There was work to be done, but she stopped anyway, letting go of the wheelbarrow's weight outside the stall of her mare, Fancy. Unhooking the simple latch, Lilly swung open the three-plank stall door by its diagonal cross beam and slipped inside.

Fancy was getting ready to be a mama for the very first time.

"You called, Miss Fancy?" Lilly let her gaze rake the horse's bulging belly.

The mare lifted her head for a soothing stroke between her eyes, then affectionately pressed her muzzle against Lilly's shoulder, her warm breath tickling Lilly's ear.

Fancy lipped and tugged at Lilly's braid.

"Stop that," but the words had no heat as Lilly pushed the horse's snout away gently.

The mare had been tugging Lilly's braid since they were both young fillies.

"You are worse than a schoolboy!" Lilly scolded. She inspected the mare, running her hand down her neck in gentle, rhythmic strokes. She placed a palm on the mare's belly, her gaze flicking to the hashmarks on the stall wall opposite. Each one represented a day in Fancy's gestation. Her beloved Fancy was almost a week late delivering her first foal.

A sharp rap sounded, and Lilly quickly slipped from the stall, Bandit padding behind her toward the big barn door that faced the street, already sliding open on its rail.

She met a body wrapped in a coat, hat pulled low, as the door yanked at her arm and snow sprayed into her eyes.

Danna O'Grady, Calvin's marshal, was there with her hat pulled low to shield her face and the collar of her coat pulled up. The marshal's chestnut mare snorted and shook her head, raining the accumulating snow across Lilly's boots as she pulled the door closed behind them.

Danna stomped snow from her boots and brushed wet flakes from the shoulders of her long duster and the legs of her wool trousers. Lilly admired the marshal's no-nonsense attire but couldn't quite bring herself to wear men's clothing.

"Mornin'!" Danna pushed her hat back a bit. "Snow's comin' on quick."

"Need to board this girl?" Lilly asked. The horse lipped the pocket where Lilly kept a stash of sugar cubes. She nudged the soft nose away. "Aren't you going home for Christmas?"

The marshal lived on a homestead out of town with her husband and two small daughters.

"With a storm like this, I may be needed in town—holiday or not. Especially after last year."

Lilly remembered the dust-up when a local rancher had tried to take revenge on Nick McGraw, shooting at him right on the street.

Danna tied off her horse in the aisle. "Expecting a train this morning. With half the hotel closed for repairs, we're gonna be hard pressed to find lodging for the passengers to hole up and wait out the storm. You may end up with an extra horse or two."

Lilly's neck flushed hot at the mention of the hotel. She set her jaw against the unhappy memories, refusing to let her expression change.

"The few boarding houses Calvin has will fill up quickly with this storm and the holiday," Danna said, unbuttoning a few buttons of her coat and loosening her scarf.

"I reckon." A thought struck Lilly. "It's almost Christmas, and there's no room in the Calvin inns."

One side of Danna's lips inched up. She scanned the livery, her eyes catching on a few empty stalls, then returning to her face. "You do remember where Mary and Joseph ended up?"

"I think the lesson is about making room in our hearts for the Savior." Lilly didn't want to think about opening her heart. It was still too raw. She would be alone this Christmas—the first one without Pa.

Danna didn't seem in any hurry to head back out into the snow and wind.

"You gonna be all right?" Danna tipped her head toward the lean-to Lilly used as her quarters. "You set to weather this storm?"

Lilly nodded. "I've got plenty of water, feed, and hay."

Danna sent her a pointed glance. "Wasn't asking about the animals. I know you will take good care of them. I was asking about you. You got enough food stocked for a couple of days?"

Lilly pictured the barren shelves above the dry sink.

"I'll be fine." This time the hot prickle in her eyes surprised her. It had been a long time since someone asked after her. "I'll be fine," she repeated, walking to the mare and moving to take off the girl's saddle.

"You've already got a couple of inches of snow on the roof." Danna motioned to Lilly's quarters again. "Want me to get someone to climb up there and sweep it off?"

"I'll get to it once the storm passes."

"If it piles up too much, you might get a leak—or worse."

"I know."

The list of things she'd been putting off for later just kept getting longer. At least she knew she had wood. She had bartered the use of a horse and wagon with one of the locals for cut wood for the stove. But she hadn't filled her wood bin yet. Another thing to add to the list.

Lilly moved to the horse's bridle and began unbuckling it. She tucked the horse into the nearest free stall and put the wooden bars in place. "I'll bring you back some water, Chestnut."

Danna raised one eyebrow. "I didn't know my horse had acquired a name."

Lilly flushed slightly. "I can't seem to help myself from giving them a nickname if they don't have one."

Finally, Danna headed toward the door. "You sure you don't need help?"

"I'm certain."

She'd learned independence from Pa. Or rather, living with Pa. She knew if she worked hard enough, she wouldn't need help.

Except there was a part of her lately that felt like she was being buried alive in a snowbank.

Danna turned back before she slipped through the door. "I'll check back when I can."

"It's not necessary, Marshal. I'm used to being on my own."

Danna nodded her farewell and stepped out into the wind and snow.

Lilly settled Chestnut with feed and water. Just as she was getting back into her chores, impatient thumps pounded against the door.

She left the wheelbarrow a few feet behind her and opened the door. A wiry man wearing a wrinkled black wool suit over a white shirt and a snow-dusted bowler hat stood before her.

"Ma'am," he drawled. He seemed to look through her, peering over her shoulder. "I'd like to speak to your man about renting a horse."

"The livery is not renting horses today. Not with the storm coming." She was used to strangers assuming there must be a man somewhere. She never outright lied. And tried not to let it bother her.

Bandit padded over and sat near her right boot, ears perked, eyes alert.

"The storm is why I need to get on the road immediately," he spoke slowly, as if explaining to a child. "Go fetch your husband," he ordered.

Lilly bristled but drew in a steadying breath, mustering a professional tone.

"We're closed for business. I suggest you find a room in town."

He scowled, his mustache creeping up like a caterpillar. "I aim to rent a horse," he said tightly.

"I said no."

His expression twisted into a sneer. "A girl like you probably can't tell a filly from a stallion. Does your man know you're turning away good customers?"

He moved forward as if he'd pass by her to enter the livery.

Bandit surged to his feet, growling.

The man startled and stepped back over the threshold.

Lilly acted on instinct, slipping behind the wheelbarrow, grabbing the handles, and rolling it forward across the threshold to create a barrier between them.

The wind whipped around her while the smell of manure swirled up from the wheelbarrow in a pungent cloud. Lilly tipped the wheelbarrow just enough to cause several clods of manure to fall on the man's boots.

"Oh, forgive me." Lilly tried for a bit of her father's north Georgian drawl. "This heavy wheelbarrow can be a bit unwieldy."

Bandit barked but faded back into the barn.

The man's fingers curled in tight fists, his mustache now an angry slash above his tightly pressed lips.

Unease prickled at the back of her neck. From the corner of her eye, she caught a glimpse of movement.

"Is there a problem, Lilly?" A deep baritone cut through the snowy silence.

Jakob Anderson.

Recognition flared, followed quickly by an involuntary wave of relief.

The man turned to Jakob even as Lilly caught sight of Jakob's wagon and pair of horses through the falling snow. When had he arrived? The wind must have masked the sounds of horses' hooves and jingling harnesses.

Bundled up in a tan coat and a black wool hat, covered in a layer of wet snow, he looked more like a large snowman than a successful farmer. He'd grown a beard, and it too was white with snow. His vivid blue eyes narrowed as they assessed the situation before edging his towering six-foot-four frame between Lilly and the angry man.

The man offered Jakob a strained smile.

"Finally, someone I can talk business with. Your man looks quite capable." The last words were thrown over Jakob's shoulder, aimed at Lilly, whose hands fisted at her sides.

"He's not my man."

Jakob let the sting of Lilly's rejection roll off as he used his body to block her from the man who'd looked like he was ready to take a swing at her.

Even without looking at her, Jakob felt the familiar pull of affection, an invisible cord that drew him to her. He might not be her man, but women should be treated with kindness and respect.

"You'll want to move along, sir." The man blinked up at Jakob, then scowled, but when Jakob didn't relent, he turned without another word. The fool headed down the boardwalk muttering about how he'd take his business to the other livery in town.

Leaving Jakob to face the woman he'd once wanted to marry.

Her cheeks were pink with cold, and strands of her auburn hair had escaped her braid to frame her heart-shaped face. And her green eyes flashed with challenge. He couldn't seem to look away now that the threat was gone.

"Why did you do that?" Lilly side-stepped Jakob and moved the wheelbarrow to one side of the big barn door. "I had things under control." She said the words over her shoulder as she heaved the big door all the way open.

Jakob wasn't so sure. He'd seen the wheelbarrow tip, watched the man stiffen with indignation and barely contained rage when she dumped the manure on his boots. Lilly was clever that way. When they'd been in school, kids teased Jakob for his height and awkwardness, and she'd found ways to defend him. Like putting crickets in Tommy Freedman's lunchbox. Part of him wanted to smile at this latest shenanigan, while another part wanted to scold her for provoking the man.

He realized she was standing in the open doorway with hands on her hips, waiting for his answer.

"I didn't do anything." He raised his hands, palms outward.

She seemed stumped for a moment, then sighed. Her eyes flitted over his shoulder to the pair of dark brown Morgan horses hitched to the wagon. Jakob followed her gaze to see Jorunn snort while Pia stomped and shook, rattling the harnesses and shaking off the accumulating snow.

"The storm is coming on too fast. I'd appreciate a place to keep the horses. If you've got room." The words rushed out of him, and he gave her his profile as heat crept up into his ears. All these months apart, and she still could still render him a foolish schoolboy. He ran a hand over his beard and worked to steady his heartbeat.

She nodded. "I'm surprised you came to town at all, with this weather threatening."

"I was roped into it against my better judgment," he admitted, moving to take Pia's bridle in one hand. He clucked his tongue, and the pair started walking slowly toward the stable door.

Lilly stepped to the side for him and the rig to pass by.

"It's Christmas." As if that explained everything. He felt Lilly's stare as he led the horses inside, and more words tumbled from his mouth. "I came to get sugar and flour and cinnamon for the cookies my new sister-in-law wanted to bake. Also, to pick up the gifts Mor ordered."

Lilly sniffed, and he went on, "It was foolish. I know. But Marta begged me. 'Please Jakob,'" he made his voice high in an imitation of his youngest sister. "'We can't have Christmas without cookies.'"

Lilly used her entire weight to tug the big door closed as the wagon passed inside. Was it sticking a little?

He gave a soft command, and the horses came to a stop. With the door closed, it was much quieter inside, and Lilly's voice carried.

"She won't have them now." She must've realized how sharp the words sounded, because she softened her expression. "She's still got you wrapped around her little finger."

He couldn't deny the affection he felt for his family, especially Marta.

"I should have stayed put. Albert said he's closing the General Store early, and all the boarding houses are full up."

Lilly didn't look at him as she moved behind the package-filled wagon and then near Jorum's side, where she started undoing the horse's harness. "The marshal told me. Where are you planning to stay?"

Her voice was cool. Almost stiff. The teasing Lilly of moments before had disappeared. Had she remembered how things were between them now? The awkwardness of a broken friendship?

Albert had suggested Jakob lodge here at the livery. With Lilly. The young man couldn't have known his simple suggestion would stir up such turmoil inside Jakob.

"I'll figure something out—"

"You should stay here."

Her words tumbled over his, leaving an awkward silence as they faded.

Jakob fumbled with the buckle on Pia's harness. Alone for a day or two to ride out the storm? Stuck inside the barn—or worse, her living quarters for all those hours?

"I don't think it's a good idea," he said.

Though he kept his eyes on the harness, he felt her glance like a spark across the horses' backs. "Don't be ridiculous. You can't sleep outside." She slipped the harness strap from Jorum's back. "I have my quarters, and you can bed down in your wagon out here. No one can say anything inappropriate went on."

Her tone was calm, matter-of-fact. Completely the opposite of how his stomach felt, twisted in knots.

When she glanced up at him again, he ducked his head and pulled off his stiff gloves, shoving them in his back pocket. Pretending it was his half-frozen fingers that slowed his task, not her outlandish suggestion.

Stay with Lilly.

The drumming in his chest quickened its rhythm. His mind whirled as he unbuckled the harness. He had harbored feelings for Lilly from the first moment they'd spoken. She had been his anchor in a new world when his family emigrated from Sweden and settled near Calvin. When she'd become engaged eighteen months ago, he'd distanced himself. Prayed desperately for his feelings to fade.

Now, after only a few minutes in her presence, everything he had worked so diligently to bury was rising to the surface, sharp enough to make him bleed.

Wind blasted against the stable door. His gaze snagged there.

Lilly's followed. "You cannot go back out in that blizzard, Jakob. Soon, you won't be able to see a foot in front of you."

He wouldn't risk the horses, and they both knew it. There seemed to be no other choice.

He couldn't look at her when he said, "Thank you, Lilly. You are a good friend to let me stay." There. They had been friends once. It would be enough.

Her brows drew together. "Are we still friends, Jakob? We haven't spoken in such a long time, and I . . ." Hurt chased the ghost of a smile from her face before she blanked her expression.

He had caused that hurt by his silence.

Regret thickened his throat. He rested one hand on Pia's back, waited for Lilly to meet his eyes.

"Yes, we are always friends," he said softly. Saying the words aloud, he realized they were true. He would always be her friend. "I'm sorry I didn't come after your father died." After the broken engagement, Jakob had wanted to come and see her. But he'd been exchanging letters with Astrid, and Mor had discouraged it.

"You're not the only one to blame," Lilly said softly. "I've been busy since Pa passed. We'll both forgive each other. All right?"

She didn't wait for an answer but led Jorunn to one of the empty stalls. Jakob followed her with Pia, settling her in the stall next door.

The quiet companionship he and Lilly had once shared seemed to be rekindled. Maybe he could make it enough.

He wouldn't hope for more. Never again.

Acknowledgments

I could not write without the love and support of so many. I am so grateful!

Above all, I must thank my Heavenly Father. He is my source.

To Trevor, without your constant support and belief in me, I could not do what I am doing. Also, to Nathan, Zachary, and Seth, my wonderful boys, who are turning into amazing men. And to Adalynn, my daughter, you are my sunshine. I can't forget both my parents and my parents-in-law. Your support, willingness to be uber driver for my kids, reading through early drafts, and anything else necessary has contributed more than you will ever know.

I'm amazed at the writing community that I'm so blessed to be a part of. To Susie, thank you so much for your encouragement and training that has been priceless. Also, to Lindsay, Katie, and the entire Sunrise editorial team for your polish to make this book shine. You are amazing!

I truly can't thank Lacy Williams enough for taking a chance on this amateur writer with a dream. Through this process with you, I have learned so much that I hope to carry on to many future stories.

Also, to Martha Hutchens, Wendy Klopfenstein, and Wendy

Galinetti. I have loved writing this series with you and truly can say you have become some of my closest friends through this process.

One last shout out to Cathy. You were the first to encourage me to audition for Sunrise Publishing. Thank you for your support! And also, to Deanna whose supportive feedback helped me through the audition process. Appreciate you, my friend!

And thank you, dear reader, for taking your valuable time to read Nick and Elsie's story. I hope you enjoyed their journey.

Thank you all!

Traci

USA Today bestselling author **Lacy Williams** is devoted to bringing her readers heartwarming love stories about cowboys and the women that tame them. She is the author of over fifty-five books, including the acclaimed Wind River Hearts and Sutter's Hollow series. Her books have been nominated for the RT Book Reviews' Seal of Excellence as well as finaled in RT's Reviewers' Choice Awards. She has been a puppy parent almost her whole life and often writes with one of her dogs snuggled in her lap. She is a mom of four and spends her non-writing time buried under piles of laundry and dishes.

Learn more at lacywilliams.net.

Traci Summeril is a Colorado girl who loves exploring the Rocky Mountains she calls home. She spent her childhood summers on her grandparents' ranch, where her rodeo queen grandmother taught her to ride and planted the seeds for the rugged cowboy heroes she writes today. When not writing, Traci is a music teacher and mom to four amazing kids. Discover more at www.tracisummeril.com.

Wind River
MAIL-ORDER BRIDES

USA Today Bestselling Author *Lacy Williams*

Martha Hutchens, Wendy Klopfenstein, Wendy Galinetti, Traci Summeril

In the wild and untamed landscape of old west Wyoming, the McGraw brothers navigate the challenges of ranch life, unexpected love, and the transformative power of second chances. As each mail-order bride enters their lives, these steadfast men discover that love can bloom in the most unlikely places. Love comes softly in Wind River...

We solve the problem of what we read next.   Available on Amazon

BLOOD OF KINGS: LEGENDS

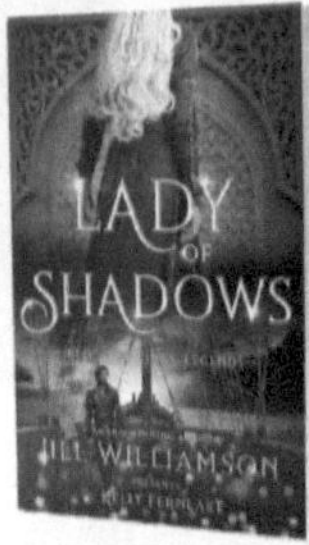

Award-winning author
JILL WILLIAMSON

with Andrew Swearingen,
Kelly Fernlake, & Niki Florica

Return to the world of Er'Rets in an epic
fantasy series brimming with richly woven
tales of loyalty, love, and sacrifice...

We solve the problem of what we read next.   Available on Amazon

YOU MAY ALSO LIKE...

When a blizzard strikes Deep Haven and Megan is overrun with catastrophes, it takes a former Ranger to step in and help. But the more he comes to her rescue, the sooner she'll move out... Come home to Deep Haven in this magical tale about the one who got away... and came back.

Still the One by **Susan May Warren and Rachel D. Russell**

Grace Howell leaves her life as a ballerina and returns to Heritage, Michigan, to heal. Teaching dance is just a temporary gig, until she finds herself unexpectedly charmed by small-town life and her growing attachment to Seth Warner, a man from her past with a troubled history of his own.

You're the Reason by **Tari Faris**

Dani Sullivan is determined to revive Jonathon Island's fading charm and reunite her fractured family. Her plan? Reopen the Grand Sullivan Hotel. But without the funds to restore the hotel, Dani's forced to accept help from Liam Stone—a big-city hotel developer whose sleek, modern vision is everything she's trying to avoid.

Meet Me at the Grand by **Lindsay Harrel**

We solve the problem of what we read next.   Available on Amazon

**WHERE EVERY STORY IS A FRIEND,
AND EVERY CHAPTER IS A NEW JOURNEY...**

Subscribe to our newsletter for a free book, the latest news, weekly giveaways, exclusive author interviews, and more!

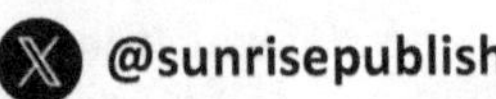

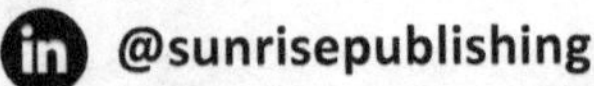

Shop paperbacks, ebooks, audiobooks, and more at
SUNRISEPUBLISHING.MYSHOPIFY.COM